THE DARKNESS OF BONES

Sam Millar's writing has been praised for its "fluency and courage of language" by Jennifer Johnson, and he has been hailed by best-selling American author Anne-Marie Duquette as "a powerful writer". He is a winner of the Martin Healy Short Story Award, the Brian Moore Award for Short Stories, the Cork *Literary Review* Competition, and the Aisling Award for Art and Culture. Born in Belfast, where he still lives, he is married and has three children. Of his first crime novel, *The Redemption Factory*, the *Irish Independent* said: "He writes well, with a certain raw energy, and he is not afraid to take risks with his fiction. The result is a novel that can sometimes be as shocking as it is original." He is also the author of one other previous novel, *Dark Souls*.

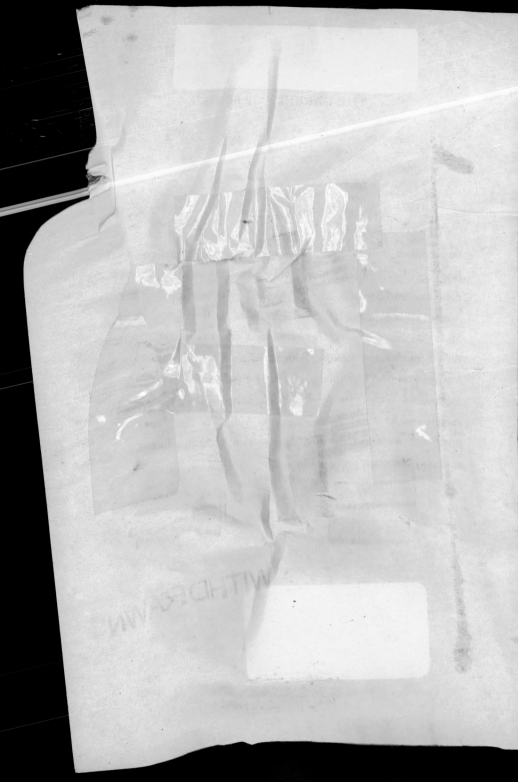

SAM MILLAR

THE DARKNESS OF BONES

A Brandon Original Paperback

First published in 2006 by
Brandon
an imprint of Mount Eagle Publications, Dingle, Co. Kerry, Ireland and
Unit 3 Olympia Trading Estate, Coburg Road, London N22 6TZ, England

2 4 6 8 10 9 7 5 3 1

ISBN 0 86322 350 8

Mount Eagle Publications/Sliabh an Fhiolair Teoranta receives support from the
Arts Council/An Chomhairle Ealaíon.

Cover design: www.designsuite.ie
Typesetting by Red Barn Publishing, Skeagh, Skibbereen
Printed in the UK

I dedicate The Darkness of Bones *to the Millen family:*
Margaret, Marcella and Paul

A person could not ask for better friends.

PART ONE

WINTER:
DARKNESS UNDER WHITENED SURFACE

" . . . the very dead of winter."
T.S. Eliot, 'Journey of the Magi'

Chapter One

"The hand of the LORD was upon me, and he brought me out by the Spirit of the LORD and set me in the middle of a valley; it was full of bones. He led me back and forth among them, and I saw a great many bones on the floor of the valley, bones that were very dry. He asked me, 'Son of man, can these bones live?'"
Ezekiel 37:1–14

ADRIAN CALVERT DISCOVERED the gruesome object less than a mile from his home, in Barton's Forest, on the outskirts of Belfast, where snow-covered trees knitted together in infinite numbers, their immensity stretching beyond the ceiling of clouds.

He should have been at school on the morning of the find, studying for an important science test, but he had taken Friday off—without permission—and had ventured into the snowy woodland because it was conveniently close to home, and could camouflage him from the prying eyes of nosy neighbours. That's all he needed: one of them squealing on him, telling his father.

Not that his father seemed to care much, these days . . .

The object protruding from the frost-covered ground resembled a grubby finger, beckoning him towards it. A beard of iced leaves hung from an old tree gone to rot, shading it from a saucer of winter sun.

Thinking at first that is was nothing more than a piece of tree root, he ignored it. But succumbing to his curiosity, he bent to inspect it further and was both startled and fascinated as he realised what it truly could be.

"A bone . . . ?"

With his fingers making contact, a spidery feeling touched his spine, alerting him to something wonderfully dark. He hoped it was some sort of fossil, but realistically believed it to be from the local butcher's, left by some scraggy mutt from town. Adrian could picture the dog digging, digging, digging, its hairy neck craning suspiciously all about as it deposited the bone in the dirty hole of earth. It probably pissed on the ground afterwards, marking its territory, fending off inquisitive, hungry adversaries.

With the heel of his shoe, he hacked determinedly at the frosted ground, fragmenting the hardened soil until the clay loosened into puckered mounds. A few minutes later, the ground grudgingly released the bone into his custody, and where the bone had rested there was now a small hollow in the earth, gaping outwards like an empty eye socket.

Studying the clay-encased bone, Adrian could see hardened blood and bluish spots of decayed meat hugging the dull paleness. "So much for you being a fossil. Probably a cow's bone." His lips curled with distaste, but still his fingers clung to the bone, resisting the urge to drop it.

Tapping it firmly against a tree, he managed to loosen as much of the stubborn clay as possible. Finally, unzipping himself, he pissed all over it, like a fireman dousing a flame, watching as his steaming urine splattered then held course, removing the last remnants of clay, blood and decomposed meat, all the while congratulating himself on his aim.

No sooner had he zipped himself up than—without warning—something hit him full force on the side of the face, knocking him off balance, forcing him to stagger, slightly.

A large crow, black and slick as oil, landed on the snowy ground beside him, thrashing its great wings, flopping on its belly. It couldn't stand and Adrian saw, for the first time, that it had only one leg. The other was gone, newly ripped from its place, possibly by a predator, leaving a mess of wet redness attached to its feathered stomach. The wetness was the only colour the bird possessed.

Instinctively raising his hand, Adrian gingerly touched his face. It was wet. Blood. Some of the crow's blood had entered his mouth. It tasted like iron on his tongue. He spat on the whitened ground, causing an inkblot of blood to discolour it a pinkish black.

Adrian wondered if the crow had been feasting on the bone, only to be ambushed by a fox. Crows were intelligent, but intelligence always paled against cunning. What if the bone was the crow's missing leg? Once again, his lips curled with distaste, yet his fingers still grasped the bone, refusing to let go.

Shaken by the eerie bird's intrusion, he shouted angrily, hoping to chase it away. "Get! Go on!" He made a movement with his hands, but the bird managed to hobble only a few inches, its energy sapped from trying to fly back to the tree for safety, its beak opening pathetically slowly, desperate for an intake of air.

"Wings are busted . . ." Remorse quickly replaced anger. Adrian considered capturing the wounded bird to bring it back home and call the animal shelter. But that would lead to questions, and he didn't need that. He wondered what his father would do in this situation. Probably put the bird out of its misery by wringing its neck.

That particular thought was unappealing—though had he brought one of his father's guns, he would have had no qualms about shooting the unfortunate creature.

Approaching the bird cautiously, Adrian tried coaxing it with his words. "It's okay; I'm not going to hurt you."

The bird remained motionless. Only when he gently touched it with his boot did he understand that it was now dying, its last effort—to seek safety—too big a strain on its heart.

Stooping slightly, he reached to roll the crow over, but its ribcage collapsed, shifting the bones grotesquely. The bird's head went lax, melting back into its feathered body.

Adrian now felt loneliness engulfing the forest. He could hear other crows cawing, nesting in the gnarled boughs of trees; he could hear the hardened snow cracking from its seams.

To his left, a small thorn tree was partially visible beneath the fattening snow. Tunnelling an opening with his hands, he placed the dying bird in, remembering how his mother always said that every creature deserved a decent burial.

Hoping that the crow's death wasn't an omen, Adrian bent and retrieved a solo black feather resting on the page of snow like an exclamation mark.

"You're a beauty. Not a blemish, despite the wound." It awed him, the feather's power and grace, its gift of flight to birds and Greek heroes. A person would sell his soul to the devil, for such . . .

A movement to his left distracted him from his thoughts. It was white—as white as the snow thickly falling all about him. Rubbing snow from his eyes, he blinked. Nothing. He glanced in every direction. Nothing, only the sly wind sounding, gathering momentum. He listened intently to the wind soughing through the trees, convinced it was whispering a name.

Michael? Michaellllll . . .?

"Spook yourself, you idiot, why don't you?" he said out loud, the sound of his voice giving him some comfort.

Quickly pocketing the feather, Adrian returned to the task of the bone, drying it with withered leaves, rubbing it almost lovingly, as if calling a sleeping genie from a magic lamp.

Satisfied, he held the bone up to the splintered light slicing through the trees, inspecting it before placing a hollow part to his ear, listening intently to the hum it made. The sound forced the hairs on his neck to prickle, and his spine to cat-scratch. He could hear the bone hiss, like a seashell; thought he could hear the sea echoing in it. Thought he could hear something else, like a sweet voice whispering dark words he couldn't understand.

Chapter Two

"THAT'S HER, ISN'T IT?" asked Joe Harris, the local barber, holding a cut-throat razor in one hand and a copy of Friday's *Belfast Telegraph* in the other. "That's Nancy McTier, the little girl who'd come in here, every now and again with her grandfather. Isn't it?" Harris mumbled the questions to himself, nudging his glasses with a knuckle to peer at the little girl's photograph stationed in the centre of the page. She was smiling and wearing a billowy dress. Ribbons rested in her hair. A toy of some sort—possibly a doll—dangled from her hand.

While studying the article, Harris neglected his third customer of the day, who sat, looking ridiculous, with only the upper lip of his face shaven.

Three years since Nancy's disappearance. No arrests. No clues. No suspects, read the tiny headline, right below the little girl's image. The article was on page thirteen of the newspaper. Three years ago, it had made page two, but time had lessened its importance. Three years from now, it probably wouldn't warrant a line.

Despite the waiting customer, it was near impossible for Harris to resist looking at the remaining random blurbs inked on the paper.

. . . walked from her home in Lancaster Street . . . the mother had given her money to buy something nice, in one of the shops in York Street . . . last seen in North Queen Street . . .

Using the endless angles afforded in the barber's shop's mirrors, the customer watched Harris, slightly concerned about the quality of the shave. But he kept quiet—for now—as if sensing the importance of the newspaper in the barber's hand.

Delving deeper into his memories of the girl, Harris conjured up sporadic images. She sometimes wore a bright yellow dress, when she came into the shop. Red butterflies attached themselves to it. The painted insects looked so real you expected them to fly away. It was a nice change, a girl, because mostly boys and men came in.

As Harris continued scanning the article, he felt the weight of the razor in his hand alerting him to his unfinished task and knew, for business' sake, he'd need to do a good job. Another one of those unisex places had recently opened a few streets away, and even though the barber's shop still managed to retain most of its loyal customers, at the back of Harris' mind was always the question as to how long they would remain loyal. Belfast was quickly becoming as bad as Dublin and London: a scarcity of traditional barbers.

The unisex shop was closed for a death in the family—hence the extra customers—and it was now up to the traditional barber's shop to take advantage of this unfortunate event.

"Sorry, sir, about that," Harris said, nodding at the article. "I remember that little girl. Terrible." He tapped the newspaper with his razor.

"I really am in a hurry," said the man, becoming slightly agitated, his partly shaven face resembling a soapy horseshoe.

Across from Harris stood Jeremiah Grazier, the other barber and owner of the shop. Grazier glared at Harris to get on with the job, satisfy the customer, and stop distracting himself with newspapers.

Grazier's body was thin and withered with time, prematurely bowed by the burden of a face deemed repulsive. He had entered this world screaming when the midwife—slightly intoxicated and inexperienced—accidentally stuck the forceps in his right eye, blinding it. The doctor casually informed Jeremiah's mother that he was lucky he hadn't lost sight in both, and recommended the placement of a glass eye, once adulthood was reached. Sometimes, when his skin got irritated, Jeremiah would be forced to wear a patch over the glass eye—though he tried to make sure this was done after working hours, kids being kids.

Grazier was preparing the hairy head of a customer, his long bony fingers massaging tonic into the hair, softening it for the scissors. The customer—a teenager—was describing the cut he wanted. Jeremiah ignored the words. There was only one hairstyle in the shop for *children*. If they wanted something *fancy*, they'd better go to one of those *fancy* salons with their *fancy* prices and *fancy* hairstylists.

Yet, despite their reluctance to change, the barbers tried as best they could to cater for all ages, and the proof was there for all to witness: homemade sweets—wrapped in a spirally red barber-pole design—were harboured in jars lining the shelves; towers of comic books were piled haphazardly, waiting to collapse; shrunken, rubber heads—meant to fascinate the younger clientele—dangled ghoulishly from the nicotined ceiling; while religious paraphernalia, consisting of old Bibles from Grazier's colporteur days, sat incongruously with magazines of half-naked women, decapitated corpses and Mafia rub-outs—appropriately enough—in barber chairs.

But if the sweets and comics were an enticement for the younger clientele, a balanced deterrent attached itself to the far wall in the curved shape of an old cane. "This Cane is Able", proclaimed the maxim beneath it, a warning to would-be troublemakers—those youngsters with the audacity to complain about the passé haircut carved on their hairy, reluctant heads.

It wasn't unusual to see Grazier chase an ungrateful boy out of the shop, the thin cane narrowly missing the head of the intended target, all the while quotes from the Bible trafficking from his aging mouth. "He that spareth the rod hateth his son! Proverbs 13–24."

If the fact of their sons' being chased by a Bible-quoting barber with a swinging cane offended the parents, they did not complain. Secretly, some of them were grateful for the old man's avenging discipline upon unruly sons—sons whom most of them found increasingly difficult to control.

"It could do with a bit more off the top, sir," said the teenager to Grazier, with respect that contradicted the barber's opinion of youth.

"Next!" shouted Grazier, ignoring the teenager's honest words.

Slithering from the chair, the teenager gingerly handed payment to the barber. In exchange, Grazier placed a perfectly wrapped sweet into the young customer's empty hand, while his words pushed him out of the shop. "Shut that door behind you, gently. Keep the heat in."

It was nearing one o'clock when the last customer finally left, granting the barbers a chance to close shop, have lunch and then clean up, ready for the two o'clock opening.

"You remember her, Jeremiah?" asked Harris, easing into one of the big fat chairs, accompanied by his newspaper, getting slowly comfortable.

"Remember who?" asked Grazier, scraping particles of hair from his clipper blades, meticulously flossing their metal teeth with his fingernails.

"That little girl—the one who disappeared? Nancy McTier. Doctor McTier's granddaughter. I know you have the worst memory in the world, but surely you remember her?"

Grazier continued his flossing, almost as if he hadn't heard Harris.

"Don't you remember her?" persisted Harris.

"Can't you see I'm busy trying to get everything in order for the two o'clock opening?" replied Grazier, sounding slightly annoyed.

Never one to listen, Harris tapped the newspaper with his finger before leaning towards the other barber. "Take a look."

Reluctantly, Grazier removed the newspaper from Harris' fingers before reading the tabloid with his good eye, like a jeweller studying the perfection of a gem.

His eye scanned the monochrome photo of the little girl before studying the words; but no matter how he tried, the photo pulled the eye back towards it, magnetically.

"Here," said Grazier, handing the newspaper back to Harris. "Disgusting stories. Don't know why you buy such trash. They only report death and destruction, making tidy profits from it, into the bargain."

Harris, well used to Grazier's sullen mood swings, simply grinned. "I remember the time when you used to go door to door with your soap, Bibles and quotes. Clean the body as well as the soul! Hallelujah! The Lord and Lard. Remember? Death and destruction? That was all I heard from you, Jeremiah. And even then you were talking about *prophets.*" Harris couldn't help but grin at the watered pun. "The sweetest-smelling Bibles known to man or *woman,* you used to tell all those old spinsters, you sly fox. Sold quite a few, too, didn't you?" Harris winked.

Grazier ignored the remarks, allowing Harris to return to his newspaper, while he went to the sink, eager to scrub the newspaper ink staining his skin. It made him feel strangely unclean.

Scrubbing thoroughly, he almost wounded his skin raw.

"Damn!"

"What? What's wrong, Jeremiah? Don't tell me you went and nicked yourself, an old pro like you?" joked Harris, never taking his eyes from the newspaper, scanning the betting pages for his daily fix from the horses. "Here's a superstitious bet, if ever I saw one. Close Shave, running at Beechmount. Seven to one. What do you think, Jeremiah? Can I entice you?"

Damn! The ink was barely fading, resisting all his efforts. He could still make out the tiny newspaper blurbs in the palm of his hand.

An insistent tapping sound from the outside window caught both Grazier's and Harris' attention, simultaneously.

"Can't they read the 'Closed for Lunch' sign? They must think we're robots," said Harris, easing from the chair.

Grazier moved quickly to intercept him.

"It's okay, Joe. You go back to your reading. I'll see who it is."

Shrugging his shoulders, Harris slipped back into his chair and returned to his newspaper.

Peeping through a side curtain, Grazier could see a young man, his face badly scarred with acne. The young man peered back, and then winked.

Reluctantly opening the door, slightly, Jeremiah hissed, "What are you doing here, in broad daylight? You were instructed to always come at night. What if someone saw you, informed the police?"

"Keep your knickers on, grandda. Just doing my job. I'm away for a couple of weeks. Your missus ordered this, yesterday. You don't want her not getting her *medicine*, do you?" His outstretched hand contained a small brown package.

An angry blood-rush pounded Jeremiah's skull. A vision entered his head, of scissors embedded in the sneering young man's mouth.

"You don't look too good, grandda. Perhaps you haven't been taking *your* medicine, lately?"

"Don't ever come to the shop at this time again," warned Jeremiah.

"Whatever you say, grandda. Just make sure you tell your missus that. See what *she* says. We all know who wears the trousers in your house." The sneer became thinner, sharper.

Speedily, Grazier took the package, squirreling it away immediately in his overcoat hanging near the entrance to the shop.

"For heaven's sake, Jeremiah. Anyone would think that was a bomb you're hiding," laughed Harris, climbing back into the comfort of the chair. "One of these days, I'm going to open that wee mystery package, Jeremiah, uncover your secret."

Without answering, Grazier stared icily at Harris. The stare was disconcerting, even to Harris.

"Joke," said Harris, quickly. "It was a joke. What's wrong with you, this weather, Jeremiah?"

For a few seconds more, Grazier continued staring before speaking. "I don't like jokes. You more than anyone should know that."

He went back to cleaning his hands.

Chapter Three

"Something dead was in each of us, and what was dead was hope."
Oscar Wilde, 'The Ballad of Reading Gaol'

EASING THROUGH THE back door of the house, Adrian made his way to the scullery. The place stank of stale smoke and decaying potatoes. Unwashed pots formed a metallic pyramid in the sink. A block of butter, touched by heat, had turned to mush.

Leaving the scullery, he turned directly left, stopping outside the large studio. Normally out of bounds for Adrian, the studio was used by his father for all the paintings he worked on, mostly of naked women—models, his father called them. Initially embarrassed and slightly uncomfortable, Adrian soon succumbed to the smiling females' charm and beauty—especially the ones who remembered his name, as they passed him in the hallway or side entrance to the house.

The red "Do Not Enter. Painting in Progress" sign was on, but pressing his ear to the door, Adrian could detect no sound.

"Dad?" Adrian's eyes squinted as they tried to focus in the darkness. "Dad? Are you in here?"

The curtains remained closed from this morning, and the light from the faded afternoon dripped through, bleaching the colours from everything in the room. Only when his eyes adjusted to the dullness did Adrian notice the lump centred on the carpet.

"Dad . . .?" Quickly pulling the curtains open, Adrian allowed the remainder of the evening to enter.

Amidst the detritus of dirty clothing looming suspiciously in corners, old newspapers—crinkled and beige from being left in the sun—carpeted the floor. Tiny mountains of clay took up a good three-quarters of sought-after space, while incomplete busts and torsos mobbed the remainder of the floor, haphazard-ly, as if an axe-murderer had recently paid a visit. A gang of meat hooks dangled ghoulishly from the ceiling like medieval torture devices, their question-mark shadows touching framed pictures of nudes.

The hum of paint was overpowering, yet Adrian could dis-tinguish two other smells far stronger—more menacing—than the paint: stale booze and fresh gun oil.

His father's body was stiff, but there was breathing. *He's out cold, that's all,* thought Adrian, relieved.

With effort, Adrian bent, attempting to pull the body from the floor, but the deadweight was too much.

"Dad? You've got to get up. C'mon!" There was annoyance in his voice. He tried again; and once again he failed to move the basking bulk. Defeated, he stood over the body. "If Mum could see you now, she'd be so ashamed. You've got to get *up!*"

Seconds later, the body moaned. "What . . . is it . . . what do . . . what do you want?" His father's voice was hoarse, uncertain.

"C'mon, Dad. Up to bed," said Adrian, pulling at his father's arm. "It's me, Adrian."

"Adrian?" There was bewilderment in the question, followed by revelation. "Oh! Adrian! Good old Adrian . . . let's have a drink to good old Adrian." The skin of his father's face was criss-crossed with carpet creases and red blotches. The face was all sharp angles and lines and, at first glance, one might have mistaken the lines for sternness.

Slowly, he moved, pushing himself up, guided by his son's pull.

"C'mon, Dad. I'll help you up the stairs."

For the first time, Adrian noticed the cherished framed photo of his mother resting on the ground, black lightning jagged across the glass, splitting her smiling face in two.

"You've busted Mum's picture," accused Adrian as he tried to suppress the bubble of anger forming in his stomach. He wanted to say drunken bastard, but something held his lips tight.

Swooning slightly, his father slowly steadied.

"You're a good son. The best son Jack Calvert could ever want," he said, patting Adrian on the cheek.

"I know. The best in the world. Now, let's be having you, Dad. You'll feel a lot better in the morning."

"A whiskey. I need a whiskey, Adrian. *That'll* make me feel a lot better—a *whole* lot better. Get me a bottle from the cupboard, will you? Just to dampen my thirst. The last few I had have all died on me." Jack winked.

"Later. Not now . . ." Not ever, he wanted to say.

Jack allowed his bodyweight to plop itself on to the old battered sofa. Closing his eyes for a few seconds, he gradually opened them before speaking. "For heaven's sake, Adrian, would you cheer up? It's Friday night. Everyone loves Friday." Then, as if a great revelation had finally revealed itself, Jack said: "Oh, now I get it. I forgot to give you your pocket money, didn't I? Get my wallet, and we'll quickly sort that out."

"Do you believe in ghosts, Dad?" asked Adrian, staring directly into his father's eyes.

Momentarily, Jack looked taken aback. Then his eyes tightened, filling with suspicion.

"I . . . that's a strange question. Why? Why . . . do you ask?"

"I think I saw Mum, out at the lake."

Silence suffocated the room. Adrian's words seemed to catch Jack in the throat, sobering him even further.

"Don't talk like that. Understand?" Jack's face reddened. "There are no ghosts. Mum is dead—something we *both* have to come to terms with."

"I saw her. She isn't dead," whispered Adrian, undeterred by his father's words. "She wouldn't do that to us. She wouldn't die, leave us all alone."

"Mum didn't do anything, Adrian. It was the drunken driver who did it. Remember? Not Mum; not you." Jack leaned towards Adrian. "When did you . . . when did you think you saw Mum?"

Remembering that he shouldn't have been in the woods that morning, Adrian carefully sidestepped the question, but accidentally revealed more about himself than he had intended. "I'm glad the drunk died, Dad. Know that? I hope he's in hell, burning. I hate him. I hope he's suffering."

Jack's face turned ashen. "It's okay to hate, son; but not forever. It only poisons, destroys. You wouldn't want Mum to see you like this. Would you?"

Releasing the tense air pocketed in his lungs, Adrian tried to sound calm, forgiving.

"No, I suppose not. I know that I shouldn't be talking like some stupid kid, but I can't help that. It's hurting me, Mum not being here."

Easing himself from the sofa, Jack gently touched Adrian's head. "You know, all the big things hurt, the things you remember. If it doesn't hurt, it's not important. Do you understand?"

Reluctantly, Adrian nodded.

Standing shakily, Jack manoeuvred towards the door. "We'll talk later, son. Okay? But for now, I'm going to take your advice and go to bed."

Less than a minute later, Adrian heard his father's body collapse on the bed above, heard the protestations from the metal springs.

Despite his efforts to ignore his hunger, Adrian's stomach rumbled loudly. He thought about going to the fridge to grab a bite, but something drew his eyes to the side of the old sofa. An object, black and lumpy. He knew what it was, even before he retrieved it: his father's revolver.

Something wasn't right. His father was strict when it came to guns, instilling in Adrian a healthy respect for them: take care of guns, and they'll take care of you.

The smell of oil on the freshly cleaned gun settled inside Adrian's nose and on the back of his throat in a clinging layer. He could taste it. He could also tell that the gun had been fired recently, could smell the burnt powder mingling with the oil.

Cautiously, holding the weapon away from his face, Adrian touched the release button, allowing the bulbous gun's stomach to reveal its gut, exposing the chambers.

Shocked at what the chamber held, Adrian tilted the gun, and a family of bullets fell harmlessly into the meat of his palm. "What are you playing at, Dad? A loaded weapon . . .?" Unpleasant thoughts entered his head, thoughts of his father doing something dark, something sinister; but these were quickly erased when he noticed the rip in the old armchair stationed beside the portable TV.

The rip—thumb-wide and finger-deep—left Adrian in no doubt of a slug housed inside the armchair.

Deciding that it was better to err on the side of caution, Adrian thought he should hide the gun. His father would need it, once he got himself back on track. Later. Certainly not now.

Climbing the stairs, he stopped outside his father's bedroom. Snores were buzzing rhythmically.

A few seconds later, he entered his own room and selected a wooden box from beneath his bed. Opening it, he deposited the gun along with the feather and bone before collapsing unceremoniously on to the bed, mentally exhausted.

His belly rumbled again, and he thought about journeying back down the stairs, grabbing a snack. Instead, he remembered the sweet, thrust into his hand by the ignorant old barber, and quickly unwrapped it before popping it in his mouth, loving the rush of sugar it sent through his body.

The winter wind was squeezing into the leaks of the old house, making him shudder as he pulled a blanket up to his chin. He felt his eyelids becoming heavier and heavier, knowing he could sleep forever, given the chance.

Eventually, he did sleep, but nightmares came rushing at him like pursuing ghosts—nightmares of all things dark and wicked: of dead mothers and dead crows; of dead bones . . .

Chapter Four

"O to be a dragon, a symbol of the power of Heaven – of silkworm size or immense; at times invisible. Felicitous phenomenon!"
Marianne Moore, *O To Be a Dragon*

ARRIVING HOME FROM work, Jeremiah fixed the key inside the lock, clicking himself into the darkness of the back kitchen. An attempted pot of stew had hardened on the stove, and the greasy aroma rushed to greet his hairy nostrils. It wasn't appetising, but Jeremiah hoped the contents would be filling.

Leaving the kitchen, a few minutes later, he went straight to the large living room, clutching the package given to him earlier that day by Harris. Glancing nervously about, he quickly placed the package behind the bookshelf, making sure that the line of books fitted back evenly.

After washing his hands, he made his way out of the house, on to the vast parcel of land.

"Judith?" he called into the darkness, knowing his wife was probably in one of the many huge sheds castled on their land. Walking down the serpentine path, he headed for the wooden buildings, passing the three scarecrows stationed together in the neglected apple-tree yard.

Some of the sheds were Aladdin's caves of discovery, filled with diverse collections of items accrued over the years; others were deserted, mere empty husks and skeleton frames of leprosy wood.

"Judith?" He opened the door of a shed, the one lodging old household utensils. Nothing. Not a sound. Then he remembered: Friday. She'd be in the clothing shed, sorting out the second-hand stuff for tomorrow's market at Smithfield. Two or more traders would call tomorrow, inspecting the goods, bartering for the best deal possible—bartering with things other than money.

The clothing shed stood head and shoulders above the cluster of other sheds, towering like a chaperone in the midst of children. But even during the day there was something unwelcoming about it.

Turning the handle of the door until it gave way, Jeremiah stepped into the large, wooden structure, dull nightlight following directly behind him.

"Judith?" he called, edging forward, cautiously. A faded orange glow emanated from a single, naked light bulb suspended from the rafters. How his wife could see in such dreadful light was beyond him. But that was how she preferred things: semi-darkness. Even the light in the house was toned down to mere shadows—shadows to help accommodate her needs. A childhood ailment was all she was willing to say, when he first met her. It had taken years for her to confide in him, reveal the real truth.

"Jud—"

"*Yesssss?* What *is* it?" hissed a harsh, annoyed voice, lurking somewhere in the semi-darkness.

"I just got in, a few minutes ago. Do . . . would you like me to put some coffee on? I brought some buns in from McKenna's Bakery."

Nothing, only a soft whispery squeal coming from the back of the shed.

"Right, then," said Jeremiah. "I'll heat the water. See you shortly?"

He left, knowing there would be no reply.

The coffee had practically turned to varnish by the time Jeremiah heard the back door creak open then shut. He could hear Judith move about restlessly, searching for something, slamming cupboards, making the cups rattle in their shelves. He knew what she was seeking, but hoped she wouldn't find it.

Less than a minute later, she appeared at the parlour door, her pale face illuminated like a ghost from the light's fading haze.

She wore a dove-grey apron over a flowery gypsy dress. The apron was speckled with large blotches the colour of parched clay, and smaller ones gleaming with new wetness. The clothes draped around her as if her bones were cradled in the very fabric, her frame emaciated with flesh barely drawing substance. Her age was half that of her husband.

"Where have you hidden it?" she asked, her voice controlled but with a hint of menace. Her eyes seemed to look at him from some point far beyond her body. Sweat beads, tiny as lice eggs, camped on her forehead.

Limiting the expressiveness of his face, Jeremiah hoped to make his response sound casual, eager to forestall any arguments.

"Hidden what?"

"*Do-not-play-fucking-games*," she hissed, each impatient and deliberate word emerging from her tight mouth. "*Where-is-my-fucking-magic-powderrrrrr!*"

Swallowing the spittle caged in his throat, Jeremiah responded. "You've used it all up. A month's supply devoured within a week. You're trying to kill yourself with all this depression and—"

"*Shut up! Shut up! Shut up!* Shut up with the fucking *preaching!* I've hardly used any! Now, where the fuck *is* it? *Where?*" She was sweating excessively now, and pressed a fist tight against her stomach as if hoping to fend off the inevitable stomach cramps starting to ferment.

Jeremiah had witnessed the telltale signs, many times, yet it always shocked him, always frightened him until he knew not what to do.

Judith's voice rose in halting queries, while Jeremiah's voice—calm but urgent—flowed insistently over and around her sharp, demanding questions.

"You can't go on like this, Judith. You've got to get help." He remained seated, resisting the urge to rise. She would perceive any movement from him as a threat, and act accordingly.

"Help *me?* Help *you,* if you don't tell me where you've fucking hidden it—*now!*" she demanded, giving him a withering look.

"You're not going to have your way, Judith. Not this time. I've always surrendered to—"

She squeezed her head between her hands, tight, like in a vice. "Your whingeing voice is like acid, going through me like diafuckingrrhoea." Her hands came abruptly down, disappearing beneath the apron, moving with purpose before reappearing, clutching something between her fingers. It was a cut-throat razor, identical to the ones in the barber's shop, held in stock by a mother-of-pearl handle.

"Put that away . . . please . . . please put it away . . ." said Jeremiah, frightened, his voice barely a whisper.

Ignoring her husband, Judith drew the razor lightly over the ball of her thumb, whetting the blade, her trance-like eyes staring at him with the unblinking intensity of a cobra preparing to strike.

Slowly and deliberately, in a perverse teasing movement, she ran the evil-looking blade up and down her bare arm, testing metal against flesh—a perforated flesh, freckled with needle marks and ant-sized nicks.

"Please, Judith . . ." pleaded Jeremiah, noticing how quickly her pupils were dilating, withdrawal rapidly taking over. This was when she was at her most dangerous—drying out.

Gently, she rested the razor in the crank of her elbow, before twisting the mother-of-pearl handle, slightly, creating a line on her pale skin. The thin line whitened then turned red.

"Judith!" screamed Jeremiah, rising quickly.

"Don't," she said calmly, her voice automatic, like an answering machine. "Don't you fucking dare to come any closer." She transferred the razor to her throat, just below the jawbone where a white scar rested like a pearl necklace.

Jeremiah wished she had screamed the words, because her calmness was always menacing, a notification of something dreadful about to happen.

"Okay," he said, defeated. "You win. I'll get it from the—"

"*No!* . . . no . . . just tell me . . . just tell me where it is." Her eyes became slits of suspicion. "That's all. I only need a small hit, a little buzz. Then your Judith will be back, the way you like her—the way you *enjoy* her. Don't you want her back, your lovely Judith?" The slits were now lines of manipulation.

Resigned, Jeremiah simply sighed and nodded. "Over on the book shelf . . ."

Cautiously—her eyes never leaving her husband—Judith stepped backwards, her left hand reaching towards the shelf, tearing frantically at the books, causing them to tumble to the ground, their pages flapping like startled doves.

It was the penultimate book that revealed the hidden treasure. "*The Power and the Glory?* How original," said Judith, her voice laced with sarcasm. "Shouldn't it be *The Powder and the Glory?*"

"Having those packages brought to the shop is dangerous. Someone could alert the police. That weasel-faced youth had the audacity to bring the package to the shop in broad daylight." Jeremiah sighed wearily. "Joe is getting suspicious. You can stop this. You're a strong woman. Addiction is for the weak."

"Fuck that little insect, Joe!" She made a snorting sound with her nose, forcing snot down her nostrils. "You have the cheek to talk about weakness! You were addicted to religion and gods before I came along, before I taught you how fucking irrelevant they *all* are. Besides, I *am* weak—willingly weak—because the weak are cruel—*very* fucking cruel." Wiping the snot with her bare arm, she left a snail trail on the skin.

Jeremiah hated when she spoke like that, and felt a tiny bubble of anger threatening to surface. But he struggled to contain it, knowing she was capable of something he would not like. Resigned, he sat back in the chair.

"It's okay. I'm not going to stop you," he mumbled.

"Stop *me? Could* you? We both doubt that, don't we?" Tearing at the parcel's brown skin, Judith fumbled for the village of syringes and powder contained within, her eyes watching Jeremiah's face.

Within seconds, the powder and needles were in her hand, and she worked them expertly, giggling nervously to herself. "Heroin is a heroine. It was devised by men to destroy and enslave women. But not this woman. I do everything willingly."

Her movements made Jeremiah think of a tricoteuse clacking her needles, sitting at the guillotine, thriving on pain and suffering, throwing her head back with laughter as each head departed from its body.

Ignoring Jeremiah's accusing glare, Judith quickly attended to the task at hand, easing the needle into a pale vein. Normally, she would inject into a muscle, prolonging the rush for up to eight minutes; but he had annoyed her, the fucking sanctimonious hypocrite with his judgmental eye, and she went straight for the vein—a guaranteed instantaneous feeling of euphoria.

Licking her lips greedily, Judith felt the surge begin, flowing steadily and gaining speed, as waves of incredible comfort flooded in. The intensity of the rush caused a reddening of her skin, bringing false life and empty promise to it. Her breathing slowed severely, almost near-death in its nothingness, while the pupils of her eyes constricted to mere pinpoints, her body going limp, relaxing for the first time in hours.

Jeremiah relaxed also, knowing that the confrontation was over—at least for the next three to four hours, until the magic wore off.

Walking towards Jeremiah, Judith stopped abruptly at his back, studying him with her slow-blinking eyes.

Jeremiah could feel her shadow on the back of his neck. He imagined the bloody redness of her eyes drilling deep into his soul, searching for oily lies.

Placing her hands gently on his shoulders, Judith squeezed, massaging his aching shoulders, almost lovingly. Jeremiah's face relaxed, his back loosened. He felt tiny buzzes of electricity touch his skin. They were delicious, like a battery rejuvenating.

Now was the time to tell her.

"There was an article in today's newspaper."

He felt her hands slip from his shoulders—a specific shift in interest.

"Newspaper?" Judith turned to face him, her lips pinched, her brow wrinkling severely. She gave him the *look*—her look when he had displeased her. "I thought we agreed that you would keep away from such trash? You know how it upsets you, fills your head full of sins."

He wished he hadn't opened his mouth, now.

Judith leaned her lips to his ear. The telltale smell of vinegary residue misted from her mouth as she sniffed, suspiciously, at his neck. "I can smell body odour. You haven't washed."

His heart beat faster.

"Just my hands," confessed Jeremiah, producing the ill-washed items for her to inspect.

"Go and shower," she commanded.

Easing himself from the chair, Jeremiah was grateful to give his stomach some movement. Judith waited until Jeremiah was gone before sitting down on his chair. She could feel his heat from it, slithering up her bony arse. It disgusted her, his heat, but she did not move, fearing she would disturb the dragon seeping lovingly throughout her body.

Gently closing her eyes, she listened to the dragon's whispers. Its words were beautiful and dark…

Chapter Five

"For God will bring every work into judgement, with every secret thing, whether it be good, whether it be evil . . ."
Ecclesiastes 12: 14

RESTING IN BED, Adrian studied the bone through an old magnifying glass. He no longer believed it to be the crow's. Too large for a crow—or any other bird, for that matter.

He wondered how he could determine what kind of bone he had discovered, where it had come from. Bits of speckled darkness played games with his thoughts. What if the bone originated from human remains? Was that possible? Of course not, but there was little harm in hoping. Perhaps he could glean some information from books at the library.

A knock on the door startled him, interrupting his thoughts.

"Adrian? Are you awake? Can I come in?" asked Jack, knocking once again.

"What? Yes—no! No, hold on a sec." Hurriedly, he slid the bone beneath the sheets and placed the magnifying glass on his bedside table.

"Adrian?"

"Right! Yes, come in."

Entering the room, Jack said, "Sorry for disturbing your

Saturday morning, but I just want to apologise for last night, and for what I said, about Mum."

Adrian calmed his breathing. "It was no big deal. You were right, anyway. There are no such things as ghosts. I don't even know why I said it, now. It's embarrassing."

Jack sat down beside the hidden bone. Adrian's heart beat faster.

"We've other, more important, things to worry about, such as your exams. You know how important they are, and how Mum always wanted you to do your best?"

"I'm the top in my class at maths and science. There's no worry there."

"If you keep taking days off, there will be," said Jack. "Mister Hegarty was good enough to call this morning, *first thing*. Said he called yesterday, but there was no answer." Jack looked slightly uncomfortable. "He informed me that you missed yesterday's class—*and* the Friday before that."

Adrian felt his face redden. "I just needed some time to myself—get some thinking done."

"You don't need to take days off from school to get some thinking done. School's the best place to do your thinking. Understand?"

Adrian nodded, reluctantly. "I suppose."

Small relief lines appeared on Jack's face. "Good."

"No, it's not good, Dad. What about you, and all the drinking? Every time I come home, you're drunk."

Jack sucked in a slice of air before releasing it in crumbs. "I . . . look, Adrian, it's not as if . . . it's not as if I'm an alcoholic. It's been a long, dry spell for me . . ."

Adrian's face tightened.

"Okay. Okay," said Jack. "I'll cut down on the booze."

The words brought a smile to Adrian's face.

"Now, I'm going to put on a big fry, for both of us. No more eating out of packages," said Jack, rising, his large palms pressing down against the hidden bone.

For a heart-stopping moment, Adrian envisaged his father pulling the sheets back, revealing the secret.

Fortunately, Jack stood and then walked towards the door.

"Dad, do you know if there was ever an old abandoned graveyard, over near Barton's Forest? Or anywhere about, near there?"

"Barton's Forest? Abandoned graveyard?" Jack seemed to be thinking. "No, not to my knowledge. The nearest graveyard is Milltown Cemetery, about five miles away. But that's still in use. Why do you ask?"

"What? Oh—no, nothing, really. I have an essay due in two weeks, about old graveyards. I was just wondering." Adrian felt his face tighten with redness. He hated the thought of lying but was secretly astonished at the boldness of the lie.

Jack shook his head, seemingly amazed by the topics bestowed on his son's generation. "Graveyards? Wish I had been given subjects like that, when I was at school. When I was a kid, many moons ago, our essays were writing about an aunt or an uncle. You kids, nowadays, have it made, with such a diverse curriculum."

"I know, we have such an easy time of it," replied Adrian, sarcastically.

Opening the door, Jack stopped abruptly. "Funny, now that you mention it, I remember being told by an old wise owl that bones *are* authors."

Pushing himself up in the bed, Adrian looked slightly puzzled. "Authors? What do you mean, Dad?"

"Every one has a story to tell."

Chapter Six

THERE IS A small circular box in Judith's bedroom that she keeps in plain view, near her bedroom window. Occasionally—when doubt and weakness attempt to seep into her thoughts—she will open the box, and remove a set of Polaroid photos. The photos are of a naked child—a boy—not yet in double figures. The boy's face is partially obscured. The photos are almost black as if overexposed to light, or wrongly shot in a darkened room. Only a bold white line running up the cleft of the young boy's scalp, mimicking the rounded valley of his buttocks, plays contrast.

The photos have aged quite a lot since their original introduction, and unlike good wine, they have not aged well. Fading is entrenched—as are numerous tiny rips. Some of the rips are accidental; nervous fingers have caused others.

Even now, all these years later, Judith believes she can clearly remember the photos being shot; the quick flash prior to the photos being vomited out through the thin mouth of the camera; the hand waving the photos, drying them, spreading them on the wooden table like a game of solitaire.

She believes she can remember the boy crying, whimpering, terrified of making a noise. She believes she can remember other things, also, but prefers not to.

Perhaps it is only her imagination telling her that she can remember such fine details, but what she needs no imagination for is the smell of unwashed skin and the darkness of a room suddenly bleached white, turning her eyes to water, and the soft voice telling the young boy that it's better in the light. So much better. *Come and look at yourself. See how the skin glistens like stardust, my little bunny.*

Chapter Seven

*"The artist brings something into the world that didn't exist before,
and . . . he does it without destroying something else."*
John Updike, *Writers at Work*

"EXPRESSIONS GALLERY", READ the sign above the door. "Owner: Sarah Bryant. Auctions and viewing held daily. Original art paintings bought and sold."

Jack knew Saturday afternoon was the gallery's busiest time of day, but what he had to say to Sarah couldn't wait any longer.

The entrance door was ajar, and he entered. A few seconds later and his eyes located Sarah standing adjacent to a large painting, speaking to a Japanese man. She seemed to be hugging the frame, as if desperately wanting to be in the painting. Her body movement and beaming face said an imminent sale.

Waving at Jack, she indicted with a finger. "One minute," she mouthed, smiling.

Jack held up his hand. "No hurry," it said. Glancing quickly away, he began studying the other paintings peppered throughout the gallery.

It was less than one minute before she appeared at his side, a kiss awarded to each cheek. "Into the office, darling. Great news," she proclaimed.

"You shouldn't leave your door open like that," said Jack, annoyance in his voice. "It's an invitation to criminals. Violent crime is on the increase, and there are a lot of dangerous people out there."

"I know, but I have my own personal protection. Don't I?" Sarah smiled as she led the way down a small corridor towards her office.

Entering the office, Sarah walked to a large mahogany desk, easing out a drawer before removing a cheque.

"For you, darling." She handed Jack the cheque.

Looking at the amount, he appeared slightly rattled. "This is a wind-up. Right? All this money for that last painting of mine?"

"Less my twenty per cent, of course." Sarah replied with a businesslike smile. "This isn't a charity shop."

"Do you know how long it would have taken me to earn this sort of money as a detective?"

"Well, you're no longer a detective; you're an artist. I always advised you not to sell yourself short. I certainly won't!" She laughed a throaty laugh. "Hopefully, it will encourage you to give up that horrible private investigating and turn professional, as an artist. Now, what's the mystery you couldn't tell me on the phone, this morning?"

Jack sighed. "There's no easy way to say this, Sarah, but I don't think we can see each other for a while."

"Oh?" Sarah frowned. "May I ask why?"

"This isn't easy, but this morning I had a conversation with Adrian. It made me feel a right bastard. It was about his mother, how he misses her."

"Of course he misses his mother. What son wouldn't?"

"I've hardly spent any time with him lately. Any spare time I have, I'm with you or the business. It just isn't right."

"I know exactly what you are saying and the reason for it, but isn't it time to live again?" said Sarah. "How long are you going to use Linda's tragic death as an excuse? I'm sorry if that sounds rude and ruthless, but I've never been one for diplomacy or self-made martyrdom. Your marriage was already on the rocks when I came along. Don't forget that."

"I'm not accusing you," replied Jack, defensively.

"Sounds like it."

A strong silence sneaked between them. Sarah was the first to break its hold. "Okay. I surrender. If our relationship is making you unhappy, I'll not cause a scene. You can have your way—for now. I'll leave you alone for the next few days, see how you feel. How does that sound?"

"I really don't deserve you. Know that?"

"You've probably never uttered a truer statement, Jack Calvert." She leaned towards him, and kissed him on the lips.

Directly across the road, hidden from view, a figure watched as Jack and Sarah emerged from the gallery. Less than a minute later, Jack entered his car, hit the ignition, and then waved goodbye.

Sarah blew him a kiss, in return.

The figure's hands were balled, fingernails cutting angrily into palms. When the hands opened again, the skin was bleeding profusely.

Chapter Eight

"As a dog returneth to his vomit, so a fool returneth to his folly."
Proverbs 26: 11

B Y CONJURING UP a mental map of the forest, Adrian tried to rediscover the exact location of his find two days earlier. He failed. Too white. Too blindingly white. There was texture but no shape, like a frozen lunar landscape.

Understanding now that he hadn't a hope of finding the location, he cursed himself for not having marked the place with something to guide him back. He should have pissed his name on the area, instead of wasting it cleaning the bone, the bone he now wanted to be human. But what if there were no more bones? Even if it were human, it could have been there for hundreds of years. Couldn't it?

No. It was clothed in rotten flesh . . .

Opening a pack of cigarettes—liberated from his father's room—Adrian popped one in his mouth. He struck a match on his jeans and quickly transferred the flame to the cig, nodding to himself with satisfaction. He was the Marlboro man in the wilderness; he was Sean Connery at the casino. The cigarette made him feel older, and that's what he wanted. His father would go nuts, of course, if he thought he smoked. Guns were no problem, but cigarettes? They're deadly, his father would say, his straight face hiding the irony.

Inhaling deep within his lungs, Adrian imagined his father standing, surveying the whitened landscape, figuring out what had to be done next while he watched the dying sun reach the hills on the horizon, sliding down behind them. When the sun was half obscured, Adrian knew that he had come a very long way from the road, and that darkness was creeping in around him. Moving to leave, he thought he heard a whisper somewhere nearby.

What was that? He craned his neck slowly, feeling something touch the back of his skull. The whisper carried upon a breeze and brushed along his senses, raising the hairs on the back of his neck. Shivering, he accidentally dropped the pilfered cigarette into the snow. The snowy ground quickly devoured it.

Stillness. The whisper was gone, replaced by a stretching silence. Adrian became motionless, listening intently, but all that could be heard was the wind skimming over the hardened surface, its soft groans hissing like punctured tires.

The wind. That's all it was. Not his mother's voice asking him what on earth he was doing with a cigarette—and stolen from his father, into the bargain. Just the wind playing games, spooking him.

The night sky was surprisingly pale, and although it was semi-dark, there was a yellowish glow to it. He wished the sky was clear so that he could see the stars, the stars that had stopped his mother with a sharp intake of breath on a frosty night and left her motionless, speechless, and utterly still on their way to church, one Sunday.

He remembered how she had stood in the street, her mouth agape with awe and wonder, as if she had seen a UFO. "What is it, Mum?" he had asked, feeling uncomfortable as people walked by, looking at her—at him.

"God," she had said. Then almost prophetically: *"When you think things have become too dark in your life, Adrian, always remember that only when it is dark enough do we get to see the stars."*

Snow began falling in fat flakes and the woods around the lake became silent. A breeze turned the resting snow into quivering white sails, like invisible mice running over it. Every once in a while, Adrian could hear a branch of a tree groaning under the strain of so much snow, and the thud of snow falling to the ground from up high in the trees. Only now, at this particular time of night, could he appreciate the bleak complexity of the tree branches besieged with ice—even if they looked like an elevated bone yard to his now galvanised imagination.

Resigned to not finding the place, he backtracked over the eastern part of the wood and emerged, just where the lake began, over near Fulton's Bend. He could see a cropped-out slice of the lake, frozen, some thirty yards off in the distance, framed by withered trees bent by nature and age. His icy breath streamed each time he opened his mouth, and then paddled right back, as if seeking shelter from where it had just been evicted.

"What on earth . . .?" Stopping suddenly, Adrian thought he could see something stuck in the centre of the ice.

From the safety of the lake's lip, he stared, squinting his eyes as the full moon pushed through the night and reflected blindingly across the hardened surface. *What is it?* he wondered, squinting his eyes at the object. *A bird? A carcass of a seagull, trapped by the ice and wind?*

Probably one of the swans, though he hoped it wasn't. He didn't like to see any bird hurt, but if it came to a toss-up between gull and swan, well, he would have to vote for the swan. He still held the memory of the crow fresh in his head, the taste of its blood on his tongue.

Scurrying as close as possible, he wished he had brought his father's binoculars for a clearer view, even if they would probably afford him little at this time of night. The mist was less heavy out from under the trees, so he could see just a little bit more. Standing perfectly still, he was absorbed by the flat expanse of the lake's glassy surface. It was a clean freeze. No ripple lines scarring the surface.

"A bird. Got to be some sort of creature. What else can it be?" He was having a conversation with himself as he needled his eyes along the surface, trying to gauge its thickness.

Don't do it, a balanced voice of sanity advised him, knowing he wouldn't listen. Anyway, he hadn't come this far to be put off by common sense, as curiosity soon won over apprehension.

Cautiously, he placed his right boot on the ice, springing his knee slightly, testing the resistance. It seemed okay. Pretty solid.

Delicately standing with one half of his bodyweight resting atop the icy surface, Adrian brought the rest of his body on board and breathed a sigh of relief when he didn't go crashing through, plunging into the darkness of murky cold water beneath.

Okay. You've proven your point. If you really wanted to walk across the lake, you could. But you're too smart for that, aren't you?

Sucking in his breath, he brought his right boot forward, followed slowly by the left. He tested the ice again, slightly forcing his weight. If he fell through at this stage, it wouldn't be too bad. The water would barely reach his chest.

Easy . . . easy . . . He moved slightly, with each step gaining confidence, momentum. He wanted to giggle. Something was tickling his stomach. Adrenaline coupled with nerves.

Creeping closer, he realised it wasn't a bird. Wrong shape. Wrong everything.

Something told him to backtrack as his eyes played tricks, making the middle of the lake wobble and warp.

Steady, he encouraged, inching his way, closer and closer. *Don't be a chicken . . . don't look back.*

Cramps were beginning to plant themselves in the calves of his legs. Coupled with the cold, they made him feel as if he was walking in slow motion. But he willed himself on, knowing that shortly he would be within touching length of the object.

"Fuck the night!" He almost fell backwards, slipping on his arse. A tiny arm, protruding from the ice like a macabre handshake, invited a touch. But it was the eyes he focused on. Blue. They looked like bluebottle flies, fat and greasy, staring up at him, ready to feast on his face. He stood still, hardly daring to breathe. Then the revelation struck. "A doll? I risked my life for a stupid doll . . ."

The doll was caked in the ice like a display at a fishmonger's window. Its features were eerily human with a pallor that made him think of his mother's powdered face in the coffin.

Regaining his composure, Adrian quickly reached down, feeling the tiny hand with his fingers, the plastic round and worn smooth by the elements. He kept feeling the hand until his own fingers went numb, losing all sensation.

Without warning, the ice made a sound, a whisper. There was a movement beneath his feet as tiny fissures began to emerge, webbing out in competing directions. A sickening feeling was quickly entering his gut.

"*Oh . . . no . . .*"

Instinctively, he stepped back, but not before reaching for the arm, pulling on it forcefully as if to keep his balance.

The whooshing sound reminded him of dirty dishwater being sucked down the kitchen sink, as the doll ascended Lazarus-like from the icy enclosure, journeying with him backwards as he skidded, slip-sliding like a drunk or a clown hoping for laughs.

But there was nothing funny about landing with a thud on his arse, his unmanageable body crashing downwards on the icy surface, opening a new, gaping wound—a wound large enough to pull him in and under, startling him with its freezing touch. Within seconds, he was under the ice, and the freezing water assaulted his ears and mouth. It tasted brackish and vile.

Submerged and disorientated by the mass of filthy water, he pushed frantically at the iced ceiling, trying to get his bearings, groping in the darkness for the entrance wound, finding nothing but resistance.

Don't panic. There has to be a way out.

But his burning lungs were not part of the positive thinking as they inflated, ready to explode, contradicting his false hope.

Think, you stupid bastard!

The water came rushing up his nostrils, flooding his head. A dull drumming sound was echoing in his brain, counting down from five, mocking him.

Five . . .

Think!

Four . . .

Shut up!

Three . . .

It's over. No point in struggling. Open your mouth and let the water take you . . . He felt his body being jolted slightly by the water's undulation.

Two . . .

Directly to his left, a new colour caught his eye. It was bright, like a lamp shining through the ice, drawing him to it like a moth to a flame.

The doll floated serenely above him, like a buoy, its plastic skin aglow from the moonlight, guiding him to the blowhole. It was the spot where he had fallen through, and if not for the fact that he was so drained—physically as well as mentally—he would have laughed at the irony of it: being saved by a doll after he had tried to rescue *it*.

With a tormented howl, he emerged through the gaping hole, his mouth sucking the beautiful icy air, *suck suck sucking*, drinking the air too quickly, making his throat gag and choke.

Possessing little strength, Adrian pulled his exhausted body to the icy surface, managing to snail gingerly along the cracked lake, stopping only when solid, snowy ground was reached.

"Alive! I'm alive!"

He lay on his stomach, impervious to the cold, breathing in large pockets of air. They tasted better than any meal he had ever sampled.

Adrian knew that he had to move quickly, get home and into dry clothes, if he wanted to avoid sickness, but his eyes remained focused on an eerie figure obscured in the thickness of trees. It was a woman—of that he was almost certain—ghostly white, studying him.

He moved quickly, running as fast as he could from the cold; running from the woman in the woods.

Chapter Nine

"If we do not find anything pleasant, at least we shall find something new."
Voltaire, *Candide*

S OME PEOPLE LEARN to live with adversity—or at least to avoid compounding one problem with another. Charlie Stanton, however, was a singular failure in both regards, and tonight looked to be no different from any other unfortunate night as the wind picked up in advance of the gathering storm, and hard, dirty hail began to fall, battering the top of his balding, exposed head.

The filthy weather matched Charlie's foul mood as he reflected on this morning's takings—or lack of them. He hadn't made much money, begging outside the church, putting on his saddest face to all the Sunday worshippers. Cheap fuckdog, he had whispered as each parishioner ignored his mumblings to spare a little food for a starving man. Some bastard had the fucking cheek to hand him a tin of fucking peas. Peas! Cheap fuckdog.

Charlie's initial plan was to seek shelter in the wasteland once covered by dodgy motels, greasy cafés and iffy bars. He could remember having meals and a few drinks not too far away from where he now stood, when times were good for everyone—

especially Charlie Stanton. He could even remember visiting one of the motels—'Alexander's', it was called in those days—accompanied by a lady of the night, two days after losing his job at the docks, seeking solace in sex and booze, finding only an empty pocket when he finally awoke, alone, the lady and his wallet gone, worsening an already dire situation.

Now, all of the buildings had been transformed to ruins, their naked stomachs roofed by tin-covered wrecks of concrete and decaying brick, seemingly forgotten by everyone except the homeless and avoiders of the law. Only one building remained moderately intact, untouched by property developers or nature, looming defiantly in the background, bleak and uninviting: Graham's Orphanage.

The orphanage had been part of the town's outer landscape for decades, and had even been used as a backdrop for a Charles Dickens film. At the height of its power, it held over two hundred children, most of whom occupied the large, eel-like dormitories. Legal wrangling over ownership had prevented much-needed restoration work from being carried out, allowing the great building to decline even further.

The cold began to nip, forcing Charlie to pick up his pace. Even as he carefully avoided the slippery patches of ice and mud, his mind was preoccupied with finding shelter quickly in the old building. The booze had narrowed his memory of the filthy wasteland, and he was finding it difficult to manoeuvre and remember in the gloved darkness. The remaining cheap wine coursing through his veins granted him some warmth, but he knew it was only a matter of time before even that deserted him, leaving him to succumb to the cold.

Walking determinedly ahead, Charlie was slightly fearful of ending up like Ben Mullan, dead, his frost-riddled body discovered next to a rubbish skip on the outskirts of town, parts of his feet devoured by foxes and rats.

Quickly pulling the collar of his overcoat up to his ears, Charlie began to hum a little ditty, mocking the anxiety eating at his stomach: "When Jack Frost comes—oh the fun. He'll play mischief on everyone. He'll pinch your nose, 'cause he's so slick, but just be careful, or he'll bite off your dick . . ." Charlie grinned at the words. "Jack, you cunning bastard, you won't get—*arghhhhhh!*" He went crashing through the dilapidated basement's storm shutters, jagged wood shredding his face, spiking it with enormous splinters, banging his head on the way down.

Then darkness came . . .

How long he remained unconscious was debatable. Had he been sober, there was little doubt he would have been dead.

"Could have snapped your stupid neck," admonished Charlie, unnerved, desperately trying to orientate himself in his surroundings as he removed a match and groped to strike it. The tiny head turned the darkness white—only for a few seconds, but enough to see a rusted sign dangling on a nail, directly above his head: "Place all dirty linen in baskets provided. Divide sheets from pillowcases. Failure to do so will mean removal of all privileges."

"Yes, sir. I'll sort all that out in a minute, once I have a browse. Wouldn't want to lose privileges on my first day, sir. And you wouldn't mind kissing my smelly arse, sir?" Charlie chuckled. "You're one lucky bastard, Charlie Stanton, landing in a pile of shitty rags, breaking your fall."

Teasingly allowing the match to burn his skin, Charlie struck another one as he eased himself out of the large metal, linen basket. Old yellowed newspapers littered the floor and he quickly coned one, lighting it like a medieval torch. The air in the basement hung unnaturally, the smell reminiscent of stale tyres and cat piss. But there was another smell, a recognisable stench sitting just outside Charlie's grasp. He tried to remember, tried to call up where he had been in contact with any part of it before, but couldn't pull the random composition together.

Abruptly, his eyes caught a small movement, coming from the far corner. Rats. They seemed to be glaring at him, their yellow eyes gleaming in the semi-darkness, their sharp teeth ready for snapping.

"Get the fuck, you dirty bastards!" He swept the torch in the rats' direction, loving the power he had to make them disappear—if only until they regrouped, gathering up their courage to repel him. "I've dealt with slimier fuckers that you bastards. I'm here to stay. Now get the fuck out, and have *your* tailed arses frost-bitten!"

As he progressed onwards, fronds of filthy web brushed against his face. He set the torch on them, also, listening to their crackling, loving the power he now possessed in his new kingdom. Finally, he bent and scooped up more paper, building another, thicker torch, all the while looking about for old wooden crates—anything to start a small fire, grant some heat and protection.

Just as he bent to retrieve some kindling, he became aware of something in the far corner, jagged light encircling it. Barely hidden by the shadows, in the semi-darkness it looked like a person, genuflecting, praying.

"Who the fuck's there?" shouted Charlie, anxious. "Come on out. Don't try anything stupid. I'm armed with a knife, you bastard. Come on! Out fucking now!"

Standing there, Charlie looked thin and awkward as a

snapped-neck chicken, barely able to refrain the shite from bursting out of his skinny arse. His hands were shaking badly; so much in fact that he thought the flaming torch would drop, leaving him in total darkness with the rats. What he wouldn't give for some cheap wine, something to help calm his nerves, make his balls grow larger.

The figure refused to acknowledge Charlie's command, and the old vagrant heard sounds behind him while his imagination went into overdrive. Were there two of them, waiting to ambush, kill him for his shoes? He spun round quickly. "Back you bastard!" To his relief, a group of rats ran for cover, knocking over empty tins in their wake.

Bending down slowly, Charlie picked up a brick before inching forward, cautiously. "I've a little drop of wine here, pal. Care to share on a cold night like this? Warm you up, good and—" He flung the brick, as hard as he could. It hit something, bouncing off with force.

Hearing bones crunch, Charlie ran forward, screaming at the top of his voice, "Bastard! Bastard! Bastard!" He lunged at the figure, dropping the smouldering torch in the process.

The stench oozing from the corner was horrendous. "Oh fuck . . ." The revelation that he was now wrestling with a badly decomposed corpse made him shiver. Yet, ever the opportunist, he felt a surge of anticipation and excitement at the thought that the corpse just might be harbouring a secret—a monetary secret, a dark face of profit, something beneficial to Charlie Stanton.

Tossed to the side of the corpse, he could make out remnants of rags that probably once covered it, devoured and moulded, replaced by battalions of webs.

The corpse was nothing more than bones and fragmented skin, and he now discovered that the ghastly thing was completely naked, as if this was how it had been left. A small metal rod protruded from the anus area. It resembled some sort of metal dildo.

"Weird . . . fucking disgusting . . ." whispered Charlie, wondering if the metal was brass. Good money in brass.

Quickly sidestepping the corpse, he bent to search the pile of raggedy clothes huddled in the corner. Who knows? Perhaps the guy—was it a man?—had left something, other than a metal dick sticking out of his arse?

With expert fingers, Charlie kept searching, all the while making sure his eyes avoided the face of the corpse—or what would be left of it.

"You cheap bastard," said Charlie, a few minutes later, fully believing that luck wouldn't be in tonight. "You cheap fucking—" Only now did he have the angry courage to look at the face; only now did he see that there was no face to confront.

Buckling over, Charlie spewed out jaundice vomit that faded into pale as it hit the ground, marooning him in its island of bread-like muck.

Whatever the poor bastard did, he didn't deserve that, thought Charlie, quickly wiping the sour spillage from his mouth, pushing himself away from the scene, covered in his own vomit, wishing he were on the road, frost and snow on his face instead of being in the company of a decapitated corpse.

Chapter Ten

"There's nothing of so infinite vexation
As man's own thoughts."
John Webster, *The White Devil*

ONE OF TWO phones rang in Jack's studio as he studied a file. A woman, suspecting her husband of infidelity, had asked him to investigate, get some photos of the unfaithful spouse, if possible.

The irony of it, thought Jack.

"You lazy bastard," accused the voice at the other end, just as the receiver touched his ear. "How long does it take you to answer the fucking phone?"

"Benson?" said Jack, smiling. "You must be in trouble. What've you done?"

"Fun*eee*. Not only a private dick, but a dick comedian, as well. Have you forgotten?" asked Harry Benson, Jack's ex-partner and best friend. Getting no reply from Jack, Benson quickly cut in. "I don't believe it. He *has* forgotten. What sacrilege! Our birthright, our annual pilgrimage, our once-in-a-year chance to get the fuck out of this smelly, godforsaken town, and he's *forgotten?*"

"How could I forget something as important as fishing? I hate to disappoint you, Harry, but Adrian has a bad cold. He slipped into the lake, a couple of nights ago. Could have had a bad accident."

"Stop with the drama, Jack. We all know Adrian's as tough as his godfather. He won't let a little cold stop him."

"I'll relay your sympathy to him. But, to be honest, I'm so backlogged in cases—"

"*You're* backlogged? Since you retired, word must have leaked out to every lowlife piece of scum in town. Violent crime has risen by five per cent. I suppose you heard about that corpse discovered in the old Graham building, over near Clifton Street?"

"The abandoned orphanage? No, I haven't been able to catch up with any news lately. What happened?"

"Some old tramp, looking for free board and breakfast, got more than he bargained for yesterday in the shape of a decapitated corpse with a dildo shoved up its bony arse."

"Decapitated?" Jack shook his head. The city was paying dearly for its cultivated big-city image: big-city diseases.

"Clean as a whistle, according to Shaw. That area was supposed to have been bulldozed over years ago to make way for a new ring road, but an ownership dispute put everything on hold. Now the fucking place is nothing more than a shantytown for all the dregs of society. They're a law unto themselves, all those vagrants, and they know the law better than we do, the bastards. If you as much as sneeze at them, they scream blue bloody murder and police brutality."

Jack could hear the disdain clearly in Benson's voice. In his ex-partner's world, everything was black and white, no grey. Them and us.

"I'm sure William Wilson must have been happy with that publicity." Jack grinned, picturing the face of his ex-boss getting redder as each TV camera was stuck into it.

"The bastard is in denial," said Benson. "He's cooking the books to suit his political ambitions—the fucker."

"Now, now, now. Can't have dissension in the ranks, Detective Benson," laughed Jack. "Superintendent Wilson doesn't tolerate it. And we all know that what Superintendent Courageous doesn't tolerate, he gets rid of."

There was silence for a few moments before Benson spoke. "We should never have allowed that cowardly bastard to force you into early retirement."

"No one forced me into anything. I wanted out. Besides, it was the best thing that ever happened. Look at me now. My own business."

"Yeah, I noticed you didn't put the word 'successful' in front of that," laughed Benson.

"Don't laugh. It takes time. One day you'll be working for me," said Jack.

"A pity your name isn't Hedges. Think of all that free publicity we'd get."

They both laughed.

Jack heard Benson's weight shift in the chair. When he spoke, his voice was conspiratorial. "I've heard through the grapevine that a certain ex-detective has been seen with a well-to-do gallery owner, quite frequently."

"No wonder nothing gets solved any more. Headless bodies, and all you can think about is gossip."

"And how did the likes of you manage to meet such a class bit of ass?" quizzed Benson.

"Sarah saw one of my paintings hanging in Chester's restaurant, over on the Lisburn Road. Loved it enough to track down the handsome talent behind it," laughed Jack.

"How is my godson taking it?"

"I haven't mentioned anything to Adrian. It's not serious, anyway. It's all above board and totally professional."

"All above bed, you mean!" snorted Benson. "Of course it's *professional.* Keep telling yourself that; but just make sure you're ready next Saturday. I'll pick you and Adrian up at three in the morning. I've a great feeling in my piss that this is our year for catching a record number of—"

"You say that every year, and every year all you end up catching is a cold. There's more chance of Wilson solving the mystery in the orphanage, than us catching anything."

"Oh ye of little faith. See you next week," said Benson, ending the conversation.

Jack went back to the file on the alleged adulterous husband. He was a week behind in forwarding some information to his client. But no matter how hard he tried, all he could think about was a headless corpse.

Chapter Eleven

"See then that ye walk circumspectly, not as fools, but as wise,
Redeeming the time, because the days are evil."
Ephesians 5: 15–16

JEREMIAH ENTERED THE barber's shop, ignoring the puzzled look scribbled on his friend's face. It was unusual for Jeremiah to be late on a Monday. In fact, Harris could not remember it ever having happened.

Jeremiah looked haggard, like battered furniture showing its age. He mumbled an incoherent apology and immediately turned to a customer.

"Next, please . . ."

"What happened to you, this morning?" asked Harris, closing the shop's door for lunch. "You look like you haven't slept a wink. Bet it's that flu. Everyone seems to be getting it. You should look after yourself with vitamins. Can't go wrong with vitamins." To prove his point, Harris loaded his tongue with small, colourful pills, and then played them to his teeth, crunching on them, irritatingly loudly.

Jeremiah grimaced. "Yes . . . I think I am coming down with a touch of it."

Scooping a newspaper from the inside pocket of his coat, Harris opened it and began to scan the pages. A few seconds later, he rested the newspaper on his lap, and looked directly at Jeremiah. "I was just thinking, last night, how the killer could be here, living in our town. Scary, isn't it?"

Jeremiah sat looking vacantly into space.

"Jeremiah?"

"What?" asked Jeremiah, blinking out of the trance. "Did you say something?"

"I said it's scary to think that the killer of that little girl is here, in the town. Perhaps only a few streets away, in that boarding house."

"Why do you keep insisting that she's dead? And what makes you think that it could be someone in town?"

"I was thinking last night of some of the weirdos we have staying here, since that cheap boarding house opened up. Every lowlife and shady character resides in there. No wonder the streets aren't safe. Katrina—God rest her soul—must be spinning in her grave, seeing the town end up like this."

Jeremiah appeared no longer to be listening as he swept nests of hair into tidy neat piles, before scooping them into the plastic bin.

"I oppose the death penalty, as you well know, Jeremiah, but I would have no qualms about hanging the bastard that murdered that child. The blood knows what it needs. Blood, being blood, doesn't care if that need is violence."

"Is this going to be the topic for the rest of the day?" cut in Jeremiah, his voice sounding slightly agitated.

"Do you remember that crazy-looking fellow who came in about two weeks ago?" continued Harris. "The one who barely said a word, even when I accidentally nicked the back of his neck? No? Well, I do. He lives in that boarding house. I noticed how he couldn't even look in the mirror when I asked him if the haircut was the way he wanted it. That's a guilty conscience. Yes, sir."

Jeremiah continued sweeping.

"Let's change the conversation, Joe. I don't like to hear stories about dead or missing children. Furthermore, I don't understand why you would, either. Why are you so concerned?"

"Okay. Have it your way. C'mon, grumpy arse," said Harris, patting the barber's chair. "Sit yourself down. I'll put you in a good mood."

Reluctantly, Jeremiah rested the brush against the mirror, and eased himself into the chair.

On cue, Harris removed a steaming towel from its hothouse enclosure and wrapped it tightly against his partner's face. This was a tiny ritual they performed on each other, usually at night after the last customer had been pruned. If done correctly, it was better than a massage.

"I can do it myself, Joe. I don't want you missing your precious horses. I should have been here, this morning."

"Give it a rest. Shut your mouth and relax. Anyway, I won't be in tomorrow. It's Katrina's anniversary. I'll be at the graveyard for most of the day, clearing up any weeds. I haven't been to her grave lately. It must look like a jungle."

The towel felt like heaven on Jeremiah's skin as Joe patted it against the contours, forming a perfect cloth image of the face.

Jeremiah loved this part of the job. Truth be told, it was one of the highlights of his life. He could barely hear Joe's muffled voice as he felt himself slowly drifting into a semi-slumber.

"When the cops come back, I'm going to tell them my suspicions about that boarding house and all those—"

"Cops? What cops?" asked Jeremiah, his voice slightly muffled against the cloth.

"Oh, cops were here this morning. Just routine. Asking door-to-door questions about the little girl. They said they'd be back, probably during the week, to ask if you remembered anything about her. I told them that you probably couldn't remember much—if anything. The only thing you ever remember is when someone owes you money," laughed Joe.

Jeremiah's hands began to shake. He could feel the blood slipping from his skin. The face-hugging towel was suffocating him as he struggled to remove it. It felt like a snake, squeezing tightly against his neck.

Chapter Twelve

"The wrath of the lion is the wisdom of God.
The nakedness of woman is the work of God.
William Blake, *The Marriage of Heaven and Hell*

J ACK STUDIED THE painting, delighted with the progress he was making on it. Each stroke of the brush brought the mosaic tapestry to life, revealing an exotic nude comprising numerous animal and insect parts. The nude's butterfly-shaped ears protruded from black, cascading hair; the nose was a tiny field mouse twitching with delight. Even the breasts were capped with elegiac, puppy-dog eyes.

This painting was going to be special. He could see that now. Even though it was a long way from being finished, this was his best work to date.

The doorbell buzzed, interrupting his thoughts.

"Sarah?" he said, opening the front door. "What are you doing here?"

"Don't wet yourself, Jack. The look on your face isn't exactly welcoming. I came by to let you know that I'll be out of town for at least a week. Going down to Galway then Dublin to exhibit some paintings from an up-and-coming artist. Oh, and a couple from an ungrateful bastard."

Feeling slightly uncomfortable, he said, "You should have phoned, saved yourself the journey, all the way over here."

"You mean, in case Adrian saw me, the woman with horns in her head?" Sarah glared.

"No. Of course not," he lied.

"Liar. Anyway, you have the phone number for both hotels. I'm sure you still remember them? If you want to talk, just pick up the phone." She turned to leave.

"Sarah, wait." Grabbing her arm, Jack mumbled, "Come in. I'll make some coffee."

She stared at his hand, then his face, before smiling. "Sure you want me to sully your home?"

Jack nodded. "That so-called smile on your face could cut glass. You'd be good in the interrogation room."

"Don't tempt me," she said, handing him her coat.

As he fumbled with the coffee-maker, Jack was conscious of Adrian upstairs in his room, making him feel like a burglar in his own house.

"Oh, Jack . . . this is beautiful," whispered Sarah, staring at the unfinished painting. "It's amazing."

"You think so?" asked Jack.

"Think? Know. It's horrible, but beautiful."

"I guess that means you hate *and* love it?" said Jack.

"It's shocking . . . almost perverted . . . I *love* it, darling . . . God! Wait until they feast their eyes on this, down at the gallery. It's absolutely brilliant."

"I don't know about that. The greatness of any painting is measured by its ability to keep surprising, revealing something new every time we go back to look at it," said Jack, chuffed, a smile appearing on his relieved face. "Time will tell if this has any surprises or revelation for—"

"I lied to you," said Sarah.

"What?" Jack looked puzzled.

"On Saturday, I told you that if our relationship was making you unhappy, then I wouldn't cause a scene. These last three days, not seeing you, have been like three weeks." Kissing him hard on the lips, she frantically worked the buttons on his shirt, popping the reluctant ones with force.

"I just bought that shirt," he laughed, watching her frustration tear the material. A few seconds later, she worked on his belt, cursing the damn thing's awkwardness.

"Dad, I need some money for . . ." Adrian stood at the door, startling Jack.

"You know better than to barge in when the red light is on!" shouted Jack, desperately trying to regain his composure.

Adrian stared at his father, and then at Sarah.

"The red light wasn't on!" screamed Adrian, turning and slamming the door behind him.

Chapter Thirteen

"In the nightmare of the dark . . ."
W.H. Auden, "In Memory of W.B. Yeats"

JEREMIAH TRIED TO sleep, but the sounds of anguished moaning disturbed him deeply. Easing himself from his bed, he cautiously made his way along the hallway, turning left at Judith's bedroom.

His heart was thumping in his chest. Should she see him standing there, 'spying on her', there would be hell to pay. He still retained the scar of a night-time encounter when she had accused him of spying, not too long ago.

Judith shifted in the bed, tossing, mumbling incoherently. Her face was bathed in beads of sweat.

Despite his fear and weariness, Jeremiah felt his hands move towards her, desperately wanting to rouse her, free her from the nightmares he knew she was enduring.

Judith's nightmare is always the same: eyes, hundreds of them, laughing, watching, hiding the faces of their owners. She always hears a voice, telling her that tonight will be her best performance yet. The audience is full of expectations.

We do not disappoint the audience, do we?

No . . . no, sir . . .

Ever?

No . . .

Good. Time then! Let this be the performance of your life. And for your own sake, make sure it outshines last night's. Otherwise . . .

He reaches for the metal rod.

No! Please, don't . . . I was feeling sick, last night. I will be a star, tonight—every night. I promise . . .

Good, and we always keep our promises, don't we?

Yes . . . yes, always . . .

Good, he says again, swiftly bringing the rod down upon her head, smashing it like a bad tomato.

Judith jerked suddenly from her sleep, her breathing heavy, almost as if someone had placed an anvil on her chest. Her eyes darted about in the darkness, searching.

Gradually, relief seeped back on to her face. The nightmare was over for now. She lay listening to the outside noises, her nostrils capturing the residue of Jeremiah's smell. He had been in here, again, spying.

"Jeremiah?" she asked, easing from the bed.

Outside the room, Jeremiah listened to his heart thumping in his head. Would she hear him, sneaking off down the hallway, if he tried to escape?

"*Jeremiah?*" hissed Judith, impatiently. "I know you're out there, listening. Your stench has filled my room. Go and shower. *Now.*"

Obediently stepping into the shower a minute later, Jeremiah was initially shocked by the coldness. His breathing became jagged while he gritted his teeth, steeling himself as the cold water hit him square in the face and concave chest, pooling between his toes. "*Hhhhhssssssss.*" He sucked in the tight air, feeling numbness spread throughout his body. Biting down on his lower lip, he tried to prevent his teeth from chattering.

"Cold is good," said Judith, pulling the shower curtains back, making them snap like a whip. "Kills all the germs and dirty things. Isn't that right?" In her hand was a broom, the large coarse type favoured by street cleaners, its twigs protruding like lethal porcupine quills.

"*Yeessss* . . ." His teeth were chattering loudly now, uncontrollably.

"Turn your face to the wall. I don't want to look at your pathetic sneaky features."

Submissively, Jeremiah turned to his left, staring at the whiteness of the tiles. They made him think of snow. They made him think of bones.

Gently—almost motherly—Judith rested the brush's quills against his neck, adding just the right amount of pressure to pockmark the skin slightly.

Jeremiah softly shuddered with anticipation, dreading but welcoming what was coming next.

"You . . ." With slow, deliberate force, Judith scraped the brush down his back, over his buttocks, never stopping until it reached his ankles. ". . . deserve . . ." Her teeth gritted as she returned the brush to its original position, on his skinny neck. ". . . every . . ." Once again, the brush commenced its bloody journey, flaying the skin, peeling thin strips in its wake. ". . . stroke . . ."

Feeling his knees begin to wobble, Jeremiah willed them to resist. His fingernails dug into the grout between the tiles, trembling for balance. Whirls of blood stained the horrible whiteness of the shower's enclosure.

The scrubbing concluded five minutes later, leaving Jeremiah's back a gouache covered in evil-looking whiplash marks.

"Look at you," hissed Judith. "Standing there in muted

acceptance, like some wretched monk offering up his sins to a deaf god." She held the broom in her hand like a spear. It was speckled with blood, sweat, and particles of skin. "You are always paying attention but never remembering; always hearing, but never listening. I don't want you reading any more trash. Is that understood?"

Shakily, Jeremiah nodded. He was on the verge of collapsing.

"And never—*ever*—come into my room. Understand?" She placed the shaft of the broom between his sagging buttocks, allowing the wood to part the fissure of his arse slightly.

"Yes . . . yes; I understand . . . fully . . ."

Judith removed the broom, turned and left.

Easing his back against the freezing water, Jeremiah allowed it to wash away the blood. It stung like wasps and scorpions, but as his hand went to his doughy penis—to his surprise and delight . . . it was rising, just like the homemade bread his mother always made on his return home from school. Seconds later, he ejaculated, mixing his cum with his blood, watching it melt away, down into the drain, wishing his sins were so easily disposed of.

Chapter Fourteen

"Till the sun grows cold,
And the stars are old,
And the leaves of the Judgement Book unfold."
Bayard Taylor, "Bedouin Song"

"I'M LOOKING FOR books on bones," said Adrian to the young librarian behind the desk in the main library at Royal Avenue. A gaggle of people sat in chairs reading the morning newspapers, killing time, relaxing, waiting for buses to take them and their cargoes of groceries home.

"Bones? Any particular type?" asked the librarian. "Dinosaurs, you mean? We've got quite a few books about—"

"Here, love," said an old man, squeezing between Adrian and the desk, interrupting. The man appeared anxious. He handed the librarian this morning's *Irish News*. "Just to let you know, someone—not me—ripped out the coupon for the free loaf. Bloody disgrace. Left a big hole, right in the local news. Wasn't me. Just letting you know, in case someone borrows this and thinks I did it. I don't want to be fined for something I didn't—*wouldn't*—do. I come here every Tuesday. You know me. Would I do something like that?"

The librarian smiled. "Don't worry about it. I'll make a note of it. We'll try and get another one."

Returning the smile, the old man left the remnants of the newspaper on the desk before scuttling away with his bag of meagre groceries.

Adrian glanced at the butchered newspaper. Just above where the coupon had mysteriously disappeared was the partial photo of a young girl. Her left arm had been cut off—along with parts of her dress—by the coupon thief.

"Sorry about that," said the librarian, her attention back on Adrian. "Old people work themselves into such a lather over nothing. He takes that coupon every Tuesday, but we never say a thing about it. Now, what was it you were looking for? Bones, right? Dinosaurs, wasn't it?"

"Human."

"Human? *Hmm.* Let me see . . ." She hit a few buttons on the computer. The screen blinked. "We've *Forensic Anthropology for Beginners.* That sounds like a great title, doesn't it? Would you like me to see if we have it in stock, or check some other titles?"

"No, that's perfect. Just let me know if you have a copy," replied Adrian angling the newspaper slightly, getting a better view of the words. *The girl had gone missing, over three years ago . . .*

"You're in luck," said the librarian. "We've a copy on the second floor. Its reference number is 237TH."

Adrian felt his head start to throb as his eyes traced down along the little girl's right arm, down to the item attached to her hand. A doll, its features weirdly life-like, stared at him from the paper. The doll's face made him feel uncomfortable, but it was the eyes that shot into his stomach. They resembled fat bluebottle flies.

Chapter Fifteen

"A certain fox, it is said, wanted to become a wolf. Ah! who can say
why no wolf has ever craved the life of a sheep?"
Jean de la Fontaine, *Fables,* Book 7

"THE POLICE VISITED the shop yesterday morning. They asked Joe questions about that missing little girl."

Judith sat in the darkness in the corner of the room, barely visible. Jeremiah wondered if she had heard him or if she was in one of her semi-trances.

He cleared his throat.

"The police—"

"I heard you the first time."

Jeremiah shifted awkwardly on the sofa. "He said that they'd be back, to ask me some questions."

Easing herself up from the chair, Judith walked to where Jeremiah was seated. The wind outside was gathering pace, strengthening itself for an attack against the house.

"Why so worried? Are you not more intelligent than simple police officers? Their weakness is their belief in themselves, their system. But we know that is false; as false as the gods you once worshipped. Isn't that correct?" She rested her hand on his head, an anointment of her testimony.

"Yes," he whispered.

"I don't hear you."

"Yes. You're right—as always." Jeremiah's voice was shaky and weak, a stark contrast to Judith's.

"I detect doubt in your voice." The skin between her eyebrows creased into a small, angry "v". She pressed her hands more firmly against his skull, her fingers probing. "Doubt can destroy us. It is our enemy banging on the door. Are you going to let our enemy in?"

"No . . ." Jeremiah winced with pain. Her fingers were hot needles.

"Doubt is still there. I can smell it, *taste* it in my mouth." Her voice became harsh, and her fingers probed deeper. Jeremiah felt them worm their way into his brain. The pain was unbearable and lovely.

"No, there is no doubt," he finally managed to say.

Facing him, she eased his chin up, staring directly into his eyes. "I have a plan, and for that plan to succeed, you must be strong—not weak. Are you strong, Jeremiah?"

The harshness in her voice wasn't untypical, but this time it possessed a kernel of gentleness.

"What kind of a plan? What is it you want me to do? You know I'm not as strong as you—no one is."

"Do you love me?" Gently, Judith kissed him. He felt his lips burn when she pulled away.

"You know I love you. More than anything on this earth." He reached and touched her hand. "But what is the plan? What can I possibly do?"

For the next minute, Jeremiah's voice rose in halting queries, while Judith's voice, calm but urgent, flowed insistently over and around his sharp questions, wearing down his objections. Finally, he succumbed.

"Okay," he sighed. "I'll do whatever you ask."

"Whatever?"

Jeremiah nodded. "Yes. Whatever."

"Good," she whispered. "Now, listen carefully . . ."

Chapter Sixteen

"There are no whole truths; all truths are half-truths.
It is trying to treat them as whole truths that plays the devil."
Alfred North Whitehead, *Dialogues*

H E UNDERSTOOD NOW that not only had it been wrong not
to tell his father about the bone, it had also been danger-
ously wrong. He should have told of his suspicions, no matter
how ridiculous they may have seemed at the time.

It was the photo in the library the previous morning that had
finally brought him to his senses: the photo of the doll.

Still, despite the resolve to tell his father, anger in his stomach still persisted. After seeing him with that horrible woman, a
couple of days ago, Adrian had wanted to do something terrible
to her. Did she think she could take the place of his mother? If
she did, she was as stupid as she was ugly.

"Adrian?" Jack's voice called from the living room. "Is that
you?"

"I'm getting a bite to eat," replied Adrian, making a bee-
line for the strawberry jam and bread on the kitchen table. He
already had his case prepared. Once his father heard—and
saw—the facts, well, then he would have little choice other
than to investigate. His father would solve this, just like he

had numerous other cases. The police force would want him back again. Better: they would *beg* him to come back, and his father would get rid of that woman. They would be a family again.

"I need to talk to you, son," said Jack, appearing at the kitchen door.

Almost dropping the jam jar, Adrian quickly regained his composure. The picture in the library had spooked him, a little, but it was the sound of his father's voice that unnerved him the most. It was extremely solemn.

The bone. He's found the bone. He's pissed off at me. I should have told him when I had the chance. Now he'll not want to listen. He'll never trust me again.

"Look, Dad, I was going to tell you. It was just that—"

"We need to talk, in the living room." Jack turned and left.

Shit! He is so pissed at me.

Wearily, Adrian followed Jack into the living room, prepared for a good telling off.

"Dad, if you just let me explain. It's not as bad as you think. I was only—"

"Let me talk. Please. I need to say this."

Obediently, Adrian sat down opposite Jack on the sofa.

"I'm sorry, for the other night, what you saw," said Jack, his voice slightly edgy.

"The red light *wasn't* on," insisted Adrian. "I would have knocked."

"I know. I shouldn't have shouted at you . . . things happen, Adrian, spontaneous things that . . . well, just take you, there and then." Jack's face reddened. "Perhaps we should have been a bit more discreet, but sometimes it doesn't work out like that."

Tiny bats of anxiety began fluttering in Adrian's stomach.

"That woman. You . . . you're not going to let her . . . you're not going to let her try and take Mum's place? Are you?"

Shaking his head, Jack said, "Sarah doesn't want to take the place of Mum. You've got to understand that. She never once implied anything like that."

"You have to get rid of her, Dad. I don't trust her."

"You don't know her, son. Sarah is a good person. Don't try to judge someone, just because—"

Adrian's face tightened. "You mean you won't get rid of her?"

Jack shook his head. "No."

"Mum would hate you right now, bringing that woman into—"

"Enough about Mum. Enough of the guilt trip! Understand? I've crucified myself enough over Mum without you hammering the nails in further." The outburst was like a slap to Adrian's face. He reeled back from Jack's words.

"What do you mean, crucifying yourself over Mum? It wasn't your fault. It was the drunk behind the wheel. It was—"

"There is no easy way to tell you this, son," Jack swallowed hard, as if to dislodge something in his throat. "I've been torturing myself for months—deservedly so, people will say—but the time has come to face up to it."

A frown appeared on Adrian's face. He had never seen his father this way before: uncertain and anxious.

"When your . . . when Mum was killed . . . when Mum was killed and I told you that she had been killed by a drunken driver . . ."

"What? What is it, Dad?"

Jack's face had turned page-white. "The drunken driver was me . . ."

Blood was siphoning from Adrian's brain. He could see his

father's mouth moving in slow motion and saw physical words form then spill from the same dirty mouth. *The . . . Drunken . . . Driver . . . Was . . . Me . . . Me . . . Me . . .*

"Adrian? Adrian!" His father was shaking him awake. It had all been a bad dream. He was late for school. That's all.

"Dad . . . ?"

"I'm sorry, son. I just couldn't tell you. I—"

"You killed Mum . . ."

"It was an accident. I swerved to—"

"You killed her! You killed Mum so that you could be with her, that woman!"

"What? No, nothing like that. It was all a terrible accident—"

"You killed her."

"It was a tragic accident, son. Trust me. I did all that I could."

"You lied."

"I'm so sorry. If only—"

"You and Mum said to me that you would always trust me, until you had a reason not to. Remember?"

"I know what must—"

"*Remember?*"

Jack nodded, defeated. "Yes . . ."

Summoning all the force he could muster, Adrian pushed his father back against the wall.

"I will never trust you again. Keep away from me! I hate you!" Within seconds, Adrian was out the front door, running into the dying light of day.

In less than an hour, the worst storm of the decade would be upon him.

Chapter Seventeen

"But by the barber's razor best subdued."
John Milton, "Samson Agonistes"

THE BARBER'S SHOP'S lights went off—except the one in the back, where Joe and Jeremiah usually discussed business.

"That's an awful lot of money, Jeremiah." Joe smiled and passed the small package towards Jeremiah.

Jeremiah looked at Joe, then at the package. His hand didn't move.

"Here," encouraged Joe. "Stop pretending to be bashful. I know it's that pride of yours. I'm only glad to be able to help you and Judith with that little bit of financial trouble."

Reluctantly, Jeremiah's hand took the package. "I wish there was another way."

"Cut the crap," said Joe, pleasantly. "You should have come to me sooner. My bank manager wasn't too happy, though. Such short notice. Just be careful on the way home, though, with all that money. Those scumbags over at the boarding house seem to be stalking the town, more and more."

"You don't know what this means to Judith."

"Don't go all sentimental." Joe hit Jeremiah playfully on the back, before walking towards the tiny medicine cabinet. He opened it, producing a bottle of whiskey in his hand. "I don't know about you, but I feel like a good stiff one. It's been a very long day. Care for one?" he asked jokingly, knowing that Jeremiah never touched the stuff.

As expected, Jeremiah shook his head.

A family of tablets, housed in the same cabinet, followed a sip of whiskey down Joe's throat. "I tell you, Jeremiah, you can't beat vitamins for beating the flu—and a good strong whiskey doesn't disappoint, either!"

Stepping from the backroom, Jeremiah closed all the blinds, and then readied the hot towel. He fumbled at the radio dial and found a foreign jazz station. It filtered blue notes everywhere. He knew the song, but couldn't remember its title.

"Ah! My throne awaits!" said Joe with a laugh, climbing into the chair as the second whiskey slid effortlessly down his gullet. "I don't care what anyone says, Jeremiah—*this* is the life: a good shave, good friends, good whiskey."

Jeremiah did not answer, simply removed the steaming towel and placed it delicately on his friend's face.

Outside, snow was falling rapidly . . .

Chapter Eighteen

"And I looked, and behold, a pale horse:
and his name that sat on him was death,
and hell followed with him."
Revelations 6: 8

INITIALLY, ADRIAN WAS sure that the wind had been moving along quite speedily, cutting at his skin. It was strange that now, in reality, it was utterly still and his entire body felt wrong with numbness. The falling snow was thick and damp and not a particle of it was moving one way or another, as if the whole scene had been whitewashed or placed in a snow-globe.

Gradually, the snow meeting his eyes altered his perception, distorting, expanding, and diminishing distance, forcing him off the main road and along the trail that bordered the lake. Darkness was creeping all about him and panic quickly began to replace anger. There was little chance of making it back home, not in these conditions. His best chance would be old man Stapleton's barn. He wondered how far away he was from it. Could he make it there in time?

Jack had reached old man Stapleton's barn just as the snow began to fall more forcefully. He prayed to God—but mostly to his dead wife, Linda—that when he entered the old barn, he would see Adrian curled up in the corner, covered in hay. He remembered how Adrian had hidden in the barn once before, for a couple of hours, because he was ashamed of his results in a geography test.

Climbing quickly from the car, Jack shone a torch against the old building. Initial indications were not good. The dilapidated place had been boarded up and, to Jack's trained eye, there was no sign of forced entry.

Seeing no way in, he quickly ran back to the car and removed a crowbar from the boot.

Working feverishly with the crowbar, he pulled on the rusted nails and groaning wood, tearing down their resistance as if Adrian's very life depended on his success.

Be there, son. Please. For me.

"Adrian!" shouted Jack, as the wood began tearing and rusted nails went popping in the darkened air. "Are you in there, Adrian? It's me. Dad. C'mon, son. Answer me. Don't do this." The crowbar wasn't working effectively enough, and he tossed it to the snowy ground, preferring to rip at the aging wood with his bare hands.

Be there . . . be there . . .

At last, with one great pull, a small entrance was created and Jack wasted no time plunging through, ripping his clothes and skin, the beam from the torch sending rats scurrying for cover.

Through the crevices in the wooden planks came cool, dry air, smelling of darkness. And emptiness.

Jack checked the place twice, hoping for traces—anything to indicate Adrian's presence. Nothing.

Rushing outside to the car, he hit the speed dial on his mobile. Perhaps Adrian had returned home? He listened to the monotonous sound, picturing the phone in the house ringing, willing Adrian to be there, to pick it up. Adrian could call him all the murdering drunken bastards of the day. *Anything you want to call me, just be there . . .*

Instead, he got his own detached voice, saying to leave a name and number. I'll get back to you as soon as possible.

"Hello? Adrian? Are you there, son? Pick up the phone . . . please . . ." Quickly, he dialled another number, hoping that Benson would be at his desk.

Kicking the car into reverse, Jack slammed the accelerator, sending the car screaming forward, blundering into the darkness, almost hitting a tree before discovering his headlights were off.

Shaken, he willed himself steady. "Go on, kill yourself, as well . . ."

Cautiously steering the car on to the main road, he backtracked over his own tyre prints. He didn't know why, but he was heading in the direction of Barton's Forest.

Ahead but barely discernable in the blinding whiteness, the snout of the white car eased into Adrian's view. It was pale and initially he thought it a ghost. It resembled a metal pig feeding nervously at a trough as it gingerly ploughed through the snow, creating liquorice tracks in its wake.

Although the forest was dark, there was a yellowish glow to the snow as the car's headlights skidded off the surface, landing a few feet from where he hunched, tired, hungry and shivering.

"A spotlight? Police . . .?" That was it. His father had called them, sent out a search party. There was relief at being found, although he was still angry with his father; still felt a simmering hatred. Yet all he wanted at this particular moment was to be in from the cold, given some hot soup and sent to bed.

Trying to move, Adrian moaned with pain. His joints had frozen to the marrow. He felt more snow rushing against his skin, almost abrasive in its force. It quickly cocooned him, and this time the sensation was wholly different. It terrified him.

"Here . . . over here . . ." he croaked. He tried to raise his hand, but it refused to budge.

Listening, he could hear the dull sound of boots crunching on snow as a figure of a man approached.

"Dad . . .?"

The man bent down and stared into Adrian's face, as if studying an exotic insect. It was weird the way the man angled his face to get a better look.

"I've blankets in the car," said the man, easing Adrian up. "What are you doing in the forest in this weather? You could've died, right here in the snow. Do your parents know you're out in this?"

The man looked familiar, even with the snow stinging Adrian's eyes. He had met him before, but couldn't quite remember where or when. Not too long ago, perhaps?

"What's your name?" asked the man, helping Adrian into the car.

"Adri . . . Adrian," said Adrian, his teeth shattering loudly.

"Soon have you warm, Adrian. The heater will have you moving again. Don't you worry. It'll soon warm your bones."

Only now did Adrian notice the slab of linoleum stretched out in the back of the car, a shovel resting neatly on top like a rifle of a fallen solider.

Then, in a flash of clarity, he remembered where he had seen the strange-looking man before. "I remember . . . I remember where I saw you," he mumbled. The heater was on full blast, but barely making a dent in his skin.

"You do?" said the man, looking confused as he checked his rear-view mirror.

"Yes . . . my barber's had been closed . . . a death . . . you cut my hair, terribly . . . you shouted at me to close the door . . . keep the heat in . . . I remember . . . you gave me a sweet . . ."

Ever so casually, the man produced a loaded syringe and pierced the tender part of Adrian's neck.

"What was . . . why . . . why did you do that? What . . . was . . .?" Adrian's hand crawled to his neck.

"Medicine. It'll help you fight the cold. At the moment, I've got a little bit of work to do. Just close your eyes, and sleep. Soon, I'll have you home."

"What . . . what's your . . . name?" asked Adrian, his eyes becoming heavier.

"I'm your friend. Jeremiah."

Adrian felt his body go limp, boneless. His head was drifting into space. "Jeremiah? Like the bullfrog?"

Jeremiah looked puzzled.

"Bullfrog? No. The prophet . . ."

Suddenly, Jack saw the car heading towards his own, pin-balling the snow, sending large wings of slush into the air.

Swerving sharply to the right, hoping to avoid the oncoming car, Jack slammed down on the brakes.

Too late. He felt the harsh impact as the other vehicle slammed the side of his car, forcing him into a wall of snow.

Dazed and slightly bloodied, Jack slithered from the car to inspect the damage. His tail light was gone, smashed like an eggshell. "Idiot," he mumbled, as the tail-lights of the other car faded into the mouth of darkness.

Chapter Nineteen

"You are going to the woman? Do not forget the whip."
Friedrich Nietzsche, *Thus Spoke Zarathustra*

ADRIAN'S HEAD WAS throbbing. He had never touched alcohol but was certain that this was what his father meant by a hangover. Rubbing his eyelids, he crumbled the hardened crust cemented to them. It took a while for his eyes to adjust and even when they did, his surroundings were obscure.

"Where am I?" he whispered, touching his head cautiously. He tried to ease himself up, but felt lethargic, as if all the bones in his body had been removed. Fortunately, the warmth was creeping slowly up his body, winning against the cold.

To his embarrassment, he was naked, barely covered by a coarse blanket stinging his skin. *Breathe easy. That's right. Don't panic. It's the hospital. That's all. The doctor or nurse will be here in a minute. Do not panic.*

Somewhere to his right, Adrian could hear sounds. They were creepy, like crying babies, muffled and hurt. The sounds filled him with the shits. Was he in a ward—some sort of children's hospital?

"Anyone there?" he whispered.

A few seconds later, a woman appeared magically from the

shadows, like a magician. Her long fingers held a cigarette, and its glow, to a degree, exposed her face. The shadows veiled the remainder of her face, but she seemed to be studying him, just like the man had done, in the forest.

"Is . . . is this the hospital? Are . . . are you a nurse? Can you tell me where I am, please?"

She ignored him, allowing the cigarette to tumble from her fingers, before crushing it with her foot—a foot bare of sock or shoe.

"How . . . how long have I been here?" Adrian's words trailed when he noticed the item her fingers now gripped: a cut-throat razor, wet and terrifying. Blood clung to it with a thickness of jam.

It was now frighteningly plain to him that he *was* in hospital, after all—a hospital for the insane. This woman was one of the patients. She looked insane. Did she intend to kill him?

"Who . . . who *are* you? Where is the man, the one who found me, the one who called himself a prophet? Do you know him?"

There was a pane of frozen silence. The woman was studying him, like a cat within reach of a bird.

When she eventually spoke, it caused the hairs on Adrian's neck to prickle.

"A prophet?" Pulling a smile across her mouth, she whispered. "No. But I do know the devil, and he can make your eyes bleed."

Chapter Twenty

*" . . . it was the season of Darkness . . . it was the
winter of despair . . ."*
Dickens, *A Tale of Two Cities*

JACK'S EXPERIENCE HAD taught him that the first twelve
hours—not twenty-four as in the movies—were the most
critical in terms of finding and returning a missing person. And
with that fearful knowledge, he pushed his way through the
doors of the police station.

A few of the old hands greeted him as he made his way down
the corridor towards Benson's office.

The door was ajar and Jack could hear Benson's loud voice
bellowing.

"I need the report right now, Claude. You were supposed
to—" Benson stopped talking for a moment. "Listen, I don't
need your sarcastic remarks at this time of—" Benson hit a button on the phone's cradle, tapping it a few times before glancing
up at Jack. "That cantankerous old bastard, Shaw, hung up on
me. I hate him."

"No, you don't. You admire his pig-headedness."

Benson mumbled. "Coffee? There's some in the pot. Almost
fresh."

"No, thanks; I'm caffeined out. Have you heard anything yet? Did you put out the Child Rescue Alert, as I asked?"

Benson appeared uncomfortable. "Jack, I'm as concerned as you, but you know the procedure and the four key criteria for activating such an extreme measure. The only one we have is that Adrian is under sixteen."

"Wrong. Number two: a senior police officer—*you*—feels that serious harm or death may occur; number three: the child *has* been kidnapped; and four: the case has sufficient descriptive details of the missing child to justify launching the alert. Besides, as you and I both know, the four criteria are all subjective. So what's keeping you?"

Benson shook his head. "Wilson would overrule any such order. He thinks Adrian is a runaway."

"Fuck Wilson and anyone else willing to stand with him." Jack's jaws tightened. "Adrian is *not* a runaway, Harry. This is my son—*your* godson—we're talking about. Don't give me the official spin. Okay? I'm not in the mood for it."

"You know as well as I do that teens *leave* for a variety of reasons, including trouble at school, problems at home. At this stage of the game, we can't consider a more complex and sinister explanation."

"You can activate the alert when it is feared that the abducted child is in imminent danger of serious harm or death."

"Abducted?" Benson swivelled on his chair, and picked up a pen from the table. His eyes narrowed, slightly. "That's a bit extreme. Is there something you're not telling me?"

"I need you to put out that alert," reiterated Jack, ignoring Benson's question.

Shaking his head, Benson replied, "I know what must be going through your head, at the minute, but—"

"How the hell can you know what I'm going through? I'm telling you Adrian is *not* a runaway. Understand? I need that bulletin released now. Every second you waste talking shite takes him further away."

"Calm down. Okay? Have you had any arguments with him lately?"

"Will you just do this? Yes or no?" asked Jack.

Weariness crept on to Benson's face. "I'll alert all personnel, for now, instructing them to be on the lookout. But until we hear something more, that's as far as it goes. No Child Rescue Alert. Understand?"

"For now," replied Jack, the edge in his voice calming slightly.

"Good. Now it's your turn to give. You still haven't answered my question. Did you and Adrian have an argument lately? Did you mention whatshername to him? The more we know, the clearer the picture becomes. You know that more than anyone."

Jack looked beyond Benson's shoulders. Stationed on the wall was a framed photo: a grinning Benson and Jack, fishing tackle sandwiched between them.

"Sarah. Her name is Sarah, and if you must know, Adrian walked in on us."

"Walked in . . . ? You mean, in the sack?" asked Benson.

"No. Nothing like that."

"Have you considered that Adrian probably thinks Sarah is trying to take the place of Linda?"

"Yes. Of course I have. And while you sit here and do your interpretation of a psychiatrist instead of a cop, Adrian is going further down the disappearing tunnel."

"Look, Jack, I'm already on thin ice with Wilson. Even alerting personnel could see me up for insubordination. Once the old hunger hits Adrian, he'll come back. Didn't he do that shit before, a couple of years ago?"

"Harry . . ." Jack looked uncertain. "I told Adrian the truth about the crash."

All blood drained from Benson's face as he quickly rose to close the door.

"Are you fucking serious?" Benson leaned his massive frame against the door.

"I had no other choice." Jack released air from his mouth. "I couldn't live a lie any longer, not with Adrian."

"I put my job on the line to cover up for you. This is how you repay me? Are you for fucking real or what?" The blood was returning quite rapidly to Benson's skin. It had a purplish hue to it.

"I know you did, and, under the same circumstances, I would have done the same for you. But it was wrong. I should have had the balls to admit what I did, but I was a coward, and a coward's suit doesn't rest well on me."

"You should have thought about that before you got behind the wheel, Jack, over the limit; before you got me involved to cover your arse. I could lose my pension, all my retirement benefits—not forgetting that bastard Wilson hanging me by the balls, possibly jail."

"I don't need you to tell me that. I know all about the consequences of human mistakes. I've beaten myself up ever since Linda's death. She didn't even want to get in the car, but I told her not to worry, it was less than a quarter of a mile to home." Jack shook his head. "I've got to get Adrian back, Harry. It's killing me, every second not knowing where he is. I know Adrian. He wouldn't run off—not like this."

Benson closed his eyes for a few seconds. When he reopened them, he looked tired.

"Jack, you no longer *know* Adrian." Benson moved from the door. "You just told him that you killed his mother. God! C'mon, man! Adrian's angry right now, and he's going to make you pay—big time. He's going to make you sweat."

"Sweat? I've been sweating blood, Harry. There's nothing left *to* sweat—"

Without warning, the door opened, revealing an angry-looking man, large cigar trapped between his teeth. Years of overeating had made the man's ripened face run amok. There was too much flesh to help counter-balance the bloated mouth. It made his chins huge, watery and weak.

"Just what the hell are you doing in my headquarters, Calvert?" seethed Superintendent William Wilson, the cigar dancing in his mouth.

"Just visiting," replied Jack, trying to control his disdain and temper.

"You've no right to be here. Your glory days are long gone, *Mister* Calvert. My advice to you is to leave, immediately. Unless, of course, you would like to see the inside of a cell—"

Lunging at Wilson, Jack caught him tightly by the throat.

"You piece of shit. The day you're able to put me in a cell, is the day I stop breathing," he hissed, desperately trying to squeeze the lit cigar into Wilson's large mouth. Only the quick interception of Benson prevented it from travelling down Wilson's large throat.

"Get out now, while you have the chance!" roared Wilson, spitting out lumps of tobacco. "I'm going to be watching you, *Mister* Calvert! Make no mistake about it. One more slip. That's all. Then you're mine . . ."

Chapter Twenty-One

"Oh, you can't help that," said the Cat: "we're all mad here. I'm
mad. You're mad."
"How do you know I'm mad?" said Alice.
"You must be," said the Cat, "or you wouldn't have come here."
Lewis Carroll, *Alice's Adventures in Wonderland*

"ADRIAN," SHE SAID, rolling his name around in her mouth as if she liked the taste of it. "You're the beautiful boy at the lake. I saw you, wandering about, lost. You saw me. Didn't you?"

"I . . ." His mind flashed back to all those days ago, when he had almost died in the stinking icy water. "I thought you . . . I thought you were my mother. But she's dead."

Touching his face, Judith said, "You poor boy. How long has your mother been dead?"

"Almost a year." Adrian looked away from her gaze. "My father killed her. He wanted to be with someone else."

"Killed? How?" Judith's eyes glistened, slightly.

"He was driving a car. He told me someone else had killed her, a drunk from out of town. He blamed him, covered it all up . . . just to be with another woman."

Judith shook her head. "That is terrible. Did he beat you ing your skin bruised as damaged fruit? Is that why you ran

"Beat me? No . . . no, he never touched me."

"Perhaps he did—perhaps you were not aware of his touches. It can easily happen."

"I don't know what you mean." Adrian was becoming confused by the questioning.

"It's okay. We can share our secrets later." She combed his hair back with her fingers, making it stand up in black spikes.

"I have no secrets," insisted Adrian.

"We all have secrets," Judith, replied, smiling.

"How long have I been here?"

"Two days. You were very sick with a fever. You could have caught pneumonia, all alone in the snow. No one cared. But I do. If you want, I can send you home, right now. Is that what you want?"

Hesitating, Adrian mumbled, "I . . . I don't know."

"Have you ever chased the dragon?" asked Judith, tilting her head slightly.

Adrian frowned. "I don't think so. What is it? What do you mean?"

Judith smiled while removing the tin foil containing the heroin from a small wooden box, resting atop a chair. A small burner accompanied it.

Placing everything on the floor, she hunched directly beside Adrian.

"It started off in Hong Kong, long before your time." Judith spread the tin foil open, revealing the brown substance, before creating a tiny flame on the burner. "It is called *chui lung*, which means chasing the dragon. The spiralling smoke looks like a dragon's tail. Mister Spittle introduced me to it, when I was very young. He introduced me to quite a few things."

Adrian smiled uncomfortably. It sounded like she was telling him a dark fairytale.

"Who's Mister Spittle?"

"See how it slithers away?" she asked, ignoring his question.

Curious, Adrian leaned over and watched her hands. The brown powder was liquefying quite rapidly, slithering like a snake—or dragon—through the crevices of foil.

"Not everyone can chase the dragon," continued Judith. "You have to learn, have to be taught." From the same small box, Judith produced a tiny metal tube.

Adrian watched, fascinated, while Judith—tube placed between her teeth—sucked in the fumes ghosting from the tin foil, the smoke pooling around her mouth.

Scanning Judith's face, Adrian felt tiny knots inside his stomach beginning to multiply. Her face looked strange, in the darkness. It frightened and fascinated him as she leaned towards him, pressing her lips against his own, forcing them open with her tongue, exhaling the smoke into his mouth. It tasted weird; it tasted dark and forbidden.

"Inhale it, journey with it to your body, allow it to burn, make your eyes bleed . . ."

Within seconds, the smoke had coated Adrian's system and induced an involuntary paralysis of his limbs for a few heart-stopping seconds. He listened as the dragon's breath reached into his lungs and began to chant a song, silently. He tried to think what the song was, but his memory was becoming cloudy, something about a bullfrog.

"Do you miss your mother?"

His head was spinning, but in a nice way.

"Yes. Very much."

"I can be your mother," whispered Judith, her eyes dense

with concentration. "I can keep you safe; love you like you've never been loved. Would you like that?"

Words clogged in his throat while the skin on his neck tingled. The blanket slipped from his shoulders, exposing most of his nakedness. He did not try to right it, and this amazed him, the audacity of it all.

"Would you like that?" she repeated, her eyes shining all-pupil, black and dangerous, inviting him in.

"Yes," he croaked, feeling the area between his legs tighten as the blanket slipped further, completely exposing everything he possessed.

Standing, Judith stripped off all her clothes, her shadow towering over him. Within seconds, he could see the dark, hairy "v" between her legs.

Reaching towards the chair, Judith reeled in the needle, while her finger and thumb worked on the liquid-filled syringe.

"This is the queen of all dragons," she whispered, placing the needle to her left breast, tapping gently for arousal on the thimble-shaped nipple before injecting metal and liquid into it.

Adrian couldn't remember when he had felt this good. Nothing seemed to matter, as if all his problems and worries had been siphoned from him. He felt marvellous as she moved tighter towards him, opening his legs slightly with her fingers, brushing her mound of breast against his face, her nipple resting on his lip like a pebble.

"Suck," she soothed, stroking his hair lovingly. "Suck the dragon's power . . ."

Hypnotised by her words, Adrian gently sucked on the erect nipple, tasting the vinegary taste on the roof of his mouth.

"Good. Very good," she encouraged. "Suck harder. It's waiting for you. It will give you new life. It will bring you places not even an imagination can reach."

Obediently, his mouth worked harder on the nipple, like a piglet on a sow.

"Good little pig," she whispered, her breath fanning his hair away.

Adrian felt movement on his penis, like the invisible fingers of a ghost. He heard her voice vibrate through his ribcage and he wanted to die with excitement and joy as the fingers manoeuvred on his firm and slightly sticky penis, curled in its little black nest of hair.

"It's okay," she soothed, and he felt her body on top of his, sliding his stiffness into her wetness.

The veins around Judith's neck began to bulge and throb like some invisible hand was choking her. The more she pushed into him, the farther her eyes rolled back into her head and the tighter the walls of her pussy squeezed.

Adrian had never experienced anything like this. It was violent, it was beautiful, like she was giving birth to his penis, as if she wanted it to be a part of her.

Without warning, Judith steered his fingers along the curve of her buttocks, guiding them into her forbidden darkness. And just when he thought it was all over, she plunged his fingers inside her arse.

"Oh fuck, oh fuck," she moaned, and she was off again.

Had Adrian looked over to his left, just as the moon's light climbed through the window, he would have seen the prophet, studying him, his face a contortion of jealousy and hatred as he witnessed Judith orgasm for the first time.

Chapter Twenty-Two

"Even the blackest of them all, the crow,
Renders good service . . ."
Henry Wadsworth Longfellow, *Tales of a Wayside Inn:*
The Poet's Tale—The Birds of Killingworth

JACK WAS SEETHING, his hands white and trembling as he dialled the number of Benson's office.

"Benson," said the uninterested voice at the other end. "What can I do for you?"

"Do? You fuck! You can start by telling me what the fuck you're playing at, informing the media that I had an argument with Adrian." Jack held the offending newspaper article at arm's length. It was on page eight. A small, but detailed account of local teenager, Adrian Calvert, missing since Wednesday, possibly a runaway, after an argument at home.

"Jack? Jack, calm down. I didn't—"

"Don't, you fucking bastard. Don't even try that 'it wasn't me, Jack'. My son is missing and all you can do is try to cover your fat arse by leaking to the newspapers that I had an argument with Adrian? I thought I knew you, Harry. You were always rock-solid. What the fuck has happened to you in that place?"

"If you would just calm down and listen for one minute. I had to make a report to Wilson. Someone tipped him off that I had instructed all personnel to be on the lookout for Adrian. I was lucky talking my way out of it. You know the procedure better than anyone, Jack. Wilson had me by the balls."

"And you told the media that I had had an argument with Adrian? Why?"

There was a silence at the other end. Jack could hear a chair moving; he pictured Benson's enormous bulk moving uncomfortably in the chair that seemed to have shrunk over the years as he piled the weight on.

"I had no other choice. Wilson wasn't allowing any more manpower to be used on what he called everyday occurrences. Kids go missing all the time, Jack. What would the media say if they discovered we were giving preferential treatment to ex-cops? Or if they knew he was my godson? What would the fucking dogs say?"

Jack understood the logic behind Benson's argument, knew he was only doing what he thought right. Still, it galled him. He had given too many years of his life to the force to be treated like a civilian.

"Jack? You still there?"

"Just."

"My gut feeling on this is that Adrian will be back, sooner rather than later. Probably today—Saturday at the very latest."

"*Your* fat gut? Wrong answer," said Jack, slamming the phone down before making his way up the stairs, into Adrian's room.

The cop in him said he shouldn't enter the bedroom. If something had happened to Adrian, this room could be of vital importance and he was contaminating it. But the father in him won out. He couldn't wait for his old buddies to come to their senses, didn't have that luxury. He had already phoned Adrian's friends, hoping beyond hope that he was staying with them, only to be told that they hadn't seen him in a few days. Even the manager at the local Warhammer shop—Adrian's frequent hide-out—couldn't recall when he last saw him.

Stepping inside the room, Jack was amazed at how it had changed over the years. But amazement was quickly replaced by a feeling of guilt. Was it a testament to his own parental neglect that he had hardly been in this room in months? Or was it simply his granting of respect and privacy to a growing son? Super-heroes had been replaced by scantily clad women and sporting personalities. Hard-rock posters had taken the place where maps of the world had once been.

Sighing, Jack resigned himself to the task ahead, hating the thought of going through Adrian's possessions, knowing how protective his son was of his privacy. But slowly and surely the father was being replaced by the keen and relentless mind of a former detective.

Searching the wardrobe first, Jack was careful not to disturb too many items. A couple of magazines fell from a box. *Playboy*. He glanced at the pages, and couldn't prevent a wry grin from appearing on his face.

"Used to be *Batman* comics."

He wondered if Linda had ever seen the *Playboy* magazines, when she cleaned out the room. If she had, she probably wouldn't have said a word. Still, he felt slightly embarrassed, as if he had intruded on his son's most intimate thoughts.

Ducking down to peer under the bed, the stench of overripe fruit attacked Jack's nostrils. Hardened socks, discarded, rested in knots covered with dust. A sticky sweet wrapper adhered to one of the socks, like a magnet.

He shook his head. "Now, those wouldn't be tolerated by your mother, Adrian," whispered Jack, the wry smile lengthening. "Dirty mags, perhaps, but never—*ever*—dirty clothes."

Placing the dirty socks in an unused laundry basket, Jack glanced about the room, his eyes resting at a chest of drawers. Stationed atop the chest of drawers stood an impressive array of highly detailed resin models from the worlds of Warhammer. It had always baffled Jack how such tiny figures could be so beautifully painted and with such loving detail, transforming tiny pieces of metal into works of art.

Opening the drawers and searching for anything, he found little. Only crumpled-up underwear and some school ties coiled like snakes basking in the sun. There was a picture of Linda, smiling, ruffling Adrian's hair, Adrian looking embarrassed.

Jack smiled at the memory. Adrian's tenth birthday. On the back of the photo was Adrian's handwriting: *Mum, I will always love you.*

The six words were too much for Jack. Fearing an emotional breakdown, he quickly set the photo back.

"Oh, Linda, what am I going to do?"

His eyes went to the small drawer attached to the bed. The drawer blended perfectly with the bed, almost camouflaging it.

Opening it, Jack was immediately shocked at the contents. "Oh God!" His stomach went cold, and he blinked a couple of times to steady his head.

"My gun? What have you been up to, Adrian? How did . . . ?" Then something came to him; something vaguely mortifying. He remembered cleaning the gun while drinking beer and scotch, destroying his own commandments. There had been a reckless frustration in him, a frustration that bent all commonsense and prudence into a warped acceptance of intolerable conduct, shooting at the TV, narrowly missing, hitting the armchair instead. He vaguely remembered what he was shooting at: Wilson, the bastard, his face that of a politician, boasting and lying in front of the cameras that crime was down; people were safer now than ever.

Jack shook his head with embarrassment at his dangerous behaviour. As if Adrian wasn't going through enough. That's all he needed—a drunk for a father, wallowing in self-pity and cheap fucking booze, a gun dangling from his hand. A loose cannon, in more ways than one.

"If Linda could see you now. Pathetic. Useless," he mumbled, wishing for his son's footsteps to sound on the stairs outside; wanting him to kick in the door, to scream and curse at him, asking what the hell his father was doing snooping in his room.

Sitting back on the chair, Jack wondered what to do next, where to search. It was then that he saw them, as startling as spilt oil on snow, nestling in the corner of the drawer. One black. One white.

The feather and the bone.

Chapter Twenty-Three

"Discovery consists of seeing what everybody else has seen and think-ing what nobody has thought."
Albert von Szent-Gyorgyi, *The Scientist Speculates*

Opening the door of Shaw's office, Jack walked in with-out being invited.

"Ever hear of knocking?" asked Shaw, peering up from the rim of his coffee cup, his elbows a "v" on the tabletop. "I hear that you are now *persona non grata*. Are you trying to test my autonomy, get me into a quarrel with Wilson?"

"Any answers for me on that bone?" asked Jack. Impatience was gnawing at him, but he knew better than to rush or try to intimidate Shaw.

Shaw took an exaggerated sip before placing the cup down on a perfectly formed "o" branded into the wood by years of hot coffee.

"Monday mornings are bedlam here. Three murders, two *possible* suicides, and the day has barely begun; yet you want me to drop everything for one damn bone? The name is Claude, not God—though at times I have my doubts."

"Is that coffee fresh?" asked Jack, pouring some of the lethal-looking black liquid into a badly chipped and stained cup, ignor-ing Shaw's acidic tongue.

"Coffee's fine, but I can't say the same for that cup in your hand. I used it last week to extract some ghastly-looking fluid from a corpse."

Studying the contents of the cup, Jack brought it to his lips, and sipped. "Extra strong. Good. Just the way I like it." He sat down, directly facing Shaw at the opposite end of the table. "What did you find?"

"It's more complex than that. It's like art; it takes time to form a picture. You being a so-called artist should know all about that."

"Wasn't it you who once told me that every bone is an author, and that your skill has always been to read the tales of death written on the bones? Just read what it tells you, then."

"So, you did listen to me, all those times you were pretending to be asleep." A wafer-thin smile wiggled on to Shaw's face. "Almost as soon as the sun touches them, most bones start to tell their story. That's true. But it's not that simple. Except for the skull, few experts are able to distinguish between human and animal bones, with certainty. Any expert would have difficulty determining their origin."

Jack placed the cup on the table. "Modesty doesn't become you. You're not *any* old expert, Shaw. You once boasted that all you needed to decipher an entire family of murder victims was a wisdom tooth. I've given you much more than a tooth."

Shaw's smile widened, exposing ill-fitting false teeth as yellow as hardened butter.

"If a bone has a pathology that can be matched to pre-mortem records, that's a start. But it requires confirmation of human origin by applying the precipitin test. The problem is that up to ninety per cent of all remains brought to forensic anthropologists turn out to be those of animals. Sometimes, however, the bones *do* turn out to be human." Shaw brought the cup to his mouth and sipped noisily.

Jack's heart moved up a beat. He wanted to reach over and pull the cup away, fling it in the corner. "This is one of those *sometimes,* isn't it?"

"I can verify that the bone *is* human in origin, but it will take me some time to establish the primary characteristics—sex, age, height, etc.," continued Shaw. "My belief is that the bone is more than likely to be pre-pubertal."

Jack sucked a quick intake of air through his nose. *Oh lord* . . . "A child? Are you certain?"

"As certain as I can be. When we are born, the skeleton has almost three hundred and fifty bones. By the time we become an adult, we will only have two hundred and six. This is because, as we grow, some of the bones knit together to form one bone. I would say this is part of the three hundred and fifty."

"How long has the child been dead? Can you determine that?"

"The child?" asked Shaw, his forehead frowning. "The subject, you mean. Be professional, Calvert. It's a bone. No longer a child. Never allow emotion to cloud your thinking. Too damn dangerous. Anyway, there are several variables in determining how long the bone could have survived, but I have not as yet determined a time."

"What about the feather?"

Swivelling on his chair, Shaw stretched and removed a large printed drawing from a specimen drawer. "It belongs to the most intelligent of birds. *Corvidae.* Crows, to you."

"A crow?" Immediately, Jack's brain began to work. Relations and chance: were the two items related, or was it simply chance which had brought them together? He hoped for the former, but the latter seemed—for now—the most plausible. He didn't want to divert attention to a dead end, wasting precious time on a hunch rather than a principle or on a handful of ruptured assumptions where only certainties needed to be.

"You never did say where you discovered the bone. I need that information for the report," said Shaw.

Placing the cup to his lips, Jack took another brave sip from the brown substance, aware of Shaw's hawk-like gaze.

"In my son's room," he said finally, reluctantly.

Shaw said nothing, as if he hadn't heard Jack's reply.

"I've got to get going." Jack stood to go. "I suspect that bone belongs to the McTier girl, Nancy, the one who went missing three years ago."

"Until I do more tests, you can't be positive of anything related to the bone," replied Shaw, looking slightly vexed.

"My son is missing out there. A week tomorrow. He's not a runaway, Shaw. I'm going to find him. Of that I *am* positive."

"You've always lacked good judgment in certain areas, Calvert, even with your acknowledged ability. But do not allow that ability to become a *liability*."

Jack nodded. "I appreciate all that you've done, Shaw, but just for the time being, keep this between us. It's important that I get some breathing space. I'm following my instincts on this, and they have rarely let me down."

"I can't avoid the bone. I must make a report. You know that. It would be unprofessional—not to mention hot water for me with Wilson."

"How long?"

Lifting a pen from the table, Shaw tapped his teeth for a few seconds before replying. "Two days. Three at the most, provided, of course, that I can find the bone which I seem to have misplaced somewhere . . ."

"Thanks."

Shaw watched Jack walk towards the door. "What are you going to do?"

Opening the door, Jack replied, "Do? I'm going to be become very *unprofessional*. I'm going to find the remains of that *child*. Her bones will lead me to my son."

Chapter Twenty-Four

"A traveller, by the faithful hound,
Half-buried in the snow was found . . ."
Henry Wadsworth Longfellow, "Excelsior"

EASING OUT OF the car, Jack quickly scanned the vast land-scape with its colourless collage of a dying winter, trying to feel some sort of direction, feeling lost yet paradoxically belonging, as if the land had been waiting for him all these years, whittling out shadows with its knife-sharp memories.

Suddenly, it struck him—to the exclusion of all other child-hood memories—that he *had* been here before, as a child, exploring the vastness of never-stopping land, awed by the wonder and force of nature.

Under no illusions about the size of the task ahead, he tightened the hood of the windcheater close around his throat and bent into the wind, conscious of the rucksack on his back enabling the wind to make him sway like a reed.

Officially, they were on the other side of winter, when spring should be showing some telltale signs of encouragement, but there was still a nasty bite in the air, and Jack's skin felt as if a potato peeler was trying to scrape it off.

At least the hardened snow was receding. Along with some

other revelatory signs of a reluctant spring, patchy areas of unfamiliar grass and weeds were tunnelling their way to the top, enabling his footing to stay the course. At the bottom was a rock-filled creek with ice patches along the shore. Further out, the ice thinned where the water ran faster.

Just this morning, an ornithologist from the town's museum had informed him that the only place he would find a murder of crows, at this time of year, would be in the middle of—

"Barton's Forest?"

"Yes," the ornithologist had replied, somewhat puzzled but seemingly impressed by Jack's quick assertion. "How did you know?"

"A hunch. An educated guess."

Of course. It had to be Barton's Forest. It was all beginning to make sense, thought Jack, trying desperately to place the pieces of the puzzle into their right positions. He could hear Adrian's voice, lingering somewhere in the back of his skull, like a leaf from a notepad: *Dad, do you know if there was ever an old abandoned graveyard, over near Barton's Forest?*

Yesterday—shortly after talking to Shaw—Jack had called on Mister Fleming, Adrian's English teacher. No, the pupils had not been assigned any essays on graveyards. Fleming had smiled at such a bizarre question but the smile had soon faded when he noticed the storm attached to Jack's face.

Now, isolated and alone, Jack stood and observed the flat expanse of the lake's glassy surface gleaming in the distance, ice coated firmly on top like a layer of smooth metal; he thought how easily a soul could slip into the thinness of the ice, mistaking its strength and calmness.

Could this have been where Adrian had been, that night when he came home soaked and shivering? Adrian had said that he slipped over near Coldstream Dam. Had that been a lie?

Jack shuddered involuntarily and quickly banished any other negative thoughts from his head.

About to begin his journey, he saw a movement on the trees in the distance—a black vibrating friction. Hastily, he extracted the binoculars from the rucksack and tried to focus on the movement. Birds—crows?—somersaulting above the confluence of trees, finding the air current before returning to their nests, covering the treetops in blackness, as if the trees were wholly made from black feathers.

The sky beyond them was reddish with patches of purple, like torn and bruised flesh, and he tried to judge the distance and species, holding the birds in the circle of the binoculars. It was tricky, trying to measure distance accurately except by reference to something else: a solo tree, perhaps; another bird; a human.

"A mile. Has to be about a mile," he mumbled, packing the binoculars, knowing it could be well over a couple of miles where the birds nested. And what if they aren't crows? What if they are starlings, or simply—?

"Shut up! Shut the fuck up! They *are* crows, you tormenting bastard! They *are!*"

But waves of anxiety and doubt rolled through him the closer he came to the trees with their feathered lodgers. He could hear no telltale cawing, only wind and the sound of his heart thumping in his head, and already he felt the emptiness of defeat.

The intensity of the climb stole his breath, leaving him gasping for air. Exhausted, he collapsed unceremoniously close to the first group of trees, and closed his eyes. Too much liquor and too many TV dinners had taken their toll. He felt old and embarrassed at his lack of fitness. His arse was cold and numb as the dying sun set neatly behind him, his shadow an obscenely long smear of darkness.

Just as he closed his eyes for a breather, a sound roused him. At first, it sounded like dry twigs being rubbed, but the more he listened, the more he was convinced it was the language of the crows echoing between the trees, whispering secret messages to each other, alerting one another to the danger of a trespasser.

Eager now, he pushed himself up, galvanised by the sound, and followed it; its siren-like power dragging his worn-out legs. A few times, he stumbled—once upon a hidden, jagged rock, tearing his pants and skin—but still he moved with purpose, and was rewarded, a few minutes later, by kamikaze crows, swooping down perilously close to his head, attempting to chase him back from whence he had come. Defensively, they began to shit, pancake his face and clothing with their droppings, pummelling the top of his windcheater.

"That's right! Come on, you feathered bastards!" Removing the gun from inside his coat, he brandished it like a madman before firing directly into the air, deliberately missing, intentionally scaring.

It worked. Only a few brave stragglers remained while the rest flew to the summit of the trees, caw-cawing in an opera of indignation.

Slightly dazed, Jack proceeded onwards, finding himself deeper in the forest's stomach. Again he heard sounds, but this time followed by stillness. This was the sound of nothingness, as if he had suddenly stepped off the edge of the world.

Had he travelled left instead of right, he would have missed it. He later wondered what would have happened had the crows not forced his redirection. Ridiculous, of course, to believe that they had somehow purposely intended for him to find it: the carcass of a bird, perfectly shaped like a plastic toy discarded at Christmas, resting inside thorny, evergreen shrubbery.

Bending slightly—not yet touching—he simply observed the story before his eyes. The missing bone leg helped the story on. Jack imagined the dying bird being banished by the council of crows, its missing leg a liability, its oozing bloody scent an open invitation to every would-be predator and enemy from within a mile radius. The bird had probably risked the thorns, believing, rightly, that they would be a deterrent to any stalker: self-preservation—especially with death knocking on the door—being the greatest spur of all life.

"Smart little bastard!" He smiled before noticing the darkness beneath the carcass.

The bones rested upon a glove of feathers and Jack removed one cautiously, as if he were defusing a bomb. His heart beat with slight jumps as he placed the feather in a plastic ziplock, praying that Shaw would find a match with the one from Adrian's room.

Rewarding himself, Jack removed a cigarette from his top pocket, added flame, and inhaled, gratefully, allowing himself some time to think, allowing the cigarette to burn in his hand while he played out the scenario in his head.

"You *were* here, son. I know it. You probably bent down at this exact spot." A wry smile appeared on Jack's face. "Did you find this bird, wounded, hobbling about the forest? Was it you who placed it in the thorn bush for safety? What else did you do? Where did you discover the bone? C'mon, Linda, help me here."

With a Swiss army knife, he carved a marking into the tree

adjacent to the bush. A few seconds later, he removed a notepad and pen, scribbling down some information, trying to map exactly where he was. Lastly, he took a mental picture of his surroundings, wishing he had remembered to bring his camera.

There was one last thing he needed to do before heading back. He fumbled for his mobile, needing to alert Shaw that he had a feather and that it was vital to have it analysed, ASAP.

In his rush, he dropped the phone and it bounced on contact with his rugged boot, skidding off it like a skimming stone, before sliding down a small embankment of loosened rocks and hardened muck.

"Shit!" He cursed his clumsiness, blaming the fatigue settling in. Later, he would reflect on that minor incident and the major consequences it forced.

It was not a natural clearing. It was temporary, like the inhabitants. The bones were covered in decayed foliage, staining the original whiteness into a blackish green. At first, while retrieving the phone, he thought they were simply carcasses of other birds and that this particular area was a graveyard for them—one he had accidentally stumbled upon. But with the slightest tilt of his head and craning of his neck, he could see the saucer-sized piece of bone semi-hidden in the ground, protruding like a miniature moon. He knew instinctively that it was too large to be a bird's; believed it to be a human skull; knew in his heart the ownership.

He could see the bones of the skeleton waiting patiently underneath the puckered and hardened soil, waiting for this moment to tell their tale like a gathering of cairns; could see the latent brains squeezed out like toothpaste.

The laddering of the ribs was almost perfect, and the skull seemed so small that he felt he could hide it in his palm. But the rest of the skeleton—from the waist down—was violated, unmoored from any decency the earth afforded it, the clothes it had once worn now threadbare rags.

Jack stared at the small body, mangled beyond belief, but not so mangled that he couldn't tell it had belonged to a girl. There was little doubt in his mind that this was the McTiers' little girl, Nancy. The skin—what little was left—was a blue hue. The ghostly blue was there in every line of her devastated face. Those who had loved her were going to suffer grief beyond measure and there was nothing he could do to help them, knowing that he was barely able to help himself at this moment.

Not yet seven, you had hardly begun your life before it ended, thought Jack bitterly. *Who could do such a thing to a child, commit such a crime?* Especially such a crime as he knew this most certainly would be revealed as. The post-mortem would have the final say but he knew the outcome. Yes, he was very afraid that he knew, and someone would soon be knocking at the McTiers' front door, telling them what had happened to their little girl, offering condolences that meant sweet fuck all to a devastated parent.

He tried to pull his eyes from the partial face with its long dishevelled hair, but his eyes returned with a will of their own, forcing him to look. A symphony of sensations—mainly revulsion—played inside him, but he quickly pushed them away. Shaw was correct: become emotionally attached and all you will do is hinder, never solve. Be callous, detached and professional. Think analytically—and who the hell knows? You just might catch the perpetrator of this ghastly crime.

Dusk was just darkening the skyline, giving it a vague purple tinge that made the filthy dying snow look shabbier, the scene more subdued and wasted. Leaning against the tree, Jack removed another well-earned cigarette. He struck a match and its sulphur stung his nostrils. Slightly dazed by the whole experience, he inhaled, and the smoke—like his thoughts—meandered through the air, drifting lazily upward, unfettered. Only after the cigarette was finished did he make the phone call, not to Shaw but to Benson.

"Harry? No, I'm not pissed off at you. Will you stop blabbering? Shut *up!* Just listen. I need you to get a team together, along with a chopper. I think I've found the McTier girl. I'm out at Barton's Forest, at the eastern part of the lake, just where the mass of trees begins. Hurry—darkness is falling very quickly here."

That was all he said, before snapping the phone shut, chopping off Benson's hyped voice and the million questions escaping at once from his friend's eager mouth.

Initially exhausted, both mentally and physically, Jack felt strangely lucid now as he pocketed the phone, waiting for the whirl of the chopper to penetrate the sky above.

He glanced at his watch. Fifteen to twenty minutes, if luck was on his side.

Regardless of his training, he was conscious of the body, a few feet away, and knew that he should ignore it, isolate it from his mind. He tried to conjure some kind of sequence of proceedings to bring her to this moment, to trace a chronology of events that explained her disappearance. *Don't allow yourself to be sidetracked. Conscious observations might turn potentialities into actualities, and you wouldn't want that, would you? Changing probabilities? No, of course not. Too sore at the minute, cloaked in self-pity and useless to everyone—especially this little girl and your son.*

It was the body's left hand that drew his attention to the item poking slightly from a curled finger bone.

Bending slightly down, he used his pen to tease the item out carefully, spearing it with the nib.

A surge of panic rose up in his throat. It was a sweet, its wrapping badly damaged by the elements. He could make out only the slightest colour from the wrapper, faded almost white. The colour was red, swirling like a barber's pole.

Yet, despite the wrapper's wretched condition, something in his stomach told him that this was similar to the wrapper he had found in Adrian's room. The one stuck to Adrian's socks.

"Oh dear lord . . ."

This startling revelation was the final straw, and suddenly Jack Calvert could no longer contain the despair that had been building inside him; the despair he had camouflaged so well. He sobbed, bitterly and alone.

Chapter Twenty-Five

"An event has happened, upon which it is difficult to speak, and impossible to be silent."
Edmund Burke, *Trial of Warren Hastings,* Vol. 2

WHEN THE REVEREND Richard Toner, vicar at the Church of Saint James, heard about the decapitated body found at the old Graham building, his worst fears quickly came to the fore. So far, the police had not been able to identify the decapitated body, and had called on anyone with information to come forward. However, even though Richard knew that it was his Christian duty to call the police, tell them what he *thought* he suspected, he was not willing to open this particular can of worms—even for God.

The darkness of the small church was broken only by the glow of the moonlight filtering through the stained-glass windows. The smell of melting candles and incense lingered while Richard knelt, praying to God.

Statues of agonised angels with majestic faces stared down from niches, seemingly judging him with their grey, cemented eyes.

Easing himself up, he grimaced, hearing his bones crack and pop, like a breakfast cereal. Arthritis had devastated most of his body, turning the most mundane tasks into Herculean endurance tests, humbling him, making him feel like poor Job on the dunghill, making him feel like a proper shit.

"Was that God or the devil you were praying to?" asked a voice in the darkness, startling him.

"What? Who's there? What are you doing in the church?" He stumbled, slightly.

"I should ask you the same question."

Richard needed more light. His eyes could barely see in the hushed darkness. He reached for the dimmer switch.

"Don't," said the voice, calmly yet effectively, with a hint of warning in it.

The impertinence! Was it one of those wretched homeless people, one he had reported to the police for loitering in his grounds, urinating up against God's holy walls?

"How did you get in here?"

"God opened the door for me. Wasn't that sweet of him?"

"You shouldn't be in here. Tuesday nights are specifically for—"

"Those are reproductions of old masters. Aren't they incredible?" said the voice, indicating the family of paintings attached to the wall, directly above Richard's head.

"I really must ask you to leave—"

"He's my favourite. El Greco, isn't it? His models came from the lunatic asylum in Toledo and the local prison. Did you know that?"

"What is it you want?" asked Richard, nervous and annoyed.

"Think about it: all those rapists, murderers, perverts and child molesters, transformed to saints on canvas. Powerful, isn't it, the way the eye can lie?"

The blasphemous tone unnerved him more. "There is no

money in the church, at this time of night. If it's food you're after, then I do have a little"

"I know you have *a little*, Small Dickey," said the voice snidely. "We all knew . . ."

Small Dickey? Richard hadn't heard that horrible nickname in a long time—a very long time, indeed. They used to say it, whisper it behind his back, those wretched, good-for-nothing, ungrateful little bastards in their smelly rags.

"Who *are* you?"

The figure stepped from the shadows.

"Don't you recognise me, Dickey? Look closer."

For some inexplicable reason, Richard stepped back, as if a demon, a creature of the night, had come to do him wrong.

"No, I don't know you. I've never—" Could he smell alcohol from the intruder's breath? "I'm afraid I must ask you to leave, right now. If you don't, I'll have no other option than to call the police."

"Oh, I wouldn't be worrying too much about such trivial things, Dickey. You'll end up with ulcers. You wouldn't want that, would you? Besides, I'll call the police for you. Afterwards . . ."

The rock housed in the leather pouch fell like a hammer against Richard's head. Immediately he let out a howl of anguish. "Please! Please . . ." Oddly, little or no blood was released, as his hands went into defensive mode, hoping to stave off further blows.

"Does that refresh your memory, Dickey? No? Okay, try this one."

The hardened pouch cracked the side of his head, forcing him to stagger like one of the homeless drunks he detested so much. It was the third blow that sent him crashing into the open arms of a waiting saint, toppling the statue backwards, the thunderous noise absorbed by the vast emptiness of the church.

"'The ones we must keep secret, for no one else would understand.' Remember those words, Dickey?" The figure knelt down beside Richard, speaking loudly over his cries. "You remember, *now?*"

Blood trickled into the eyes of Reverend Richard Toner, vicar at the Church of Saint James, drowning them; but not before his memory came rushing back to haunt him, one last time.

Yes, he remembered—remembered all too well.

Chapter Twenty-Six

"The frost performs its secret ministry,
Unhelped by any wind."
Samuel Taylor Coleridge, "Frost at Midnight"

"HOW *LONG?*" REITERATED Jack, his voice edgy. The astringent stench of formaldehyde was beginning to make his head swoon. Lack of food in his stomach wasn't helping either.

Shrugging his shoulders, Shaw said, "Estimating the time interval since death can be extremely difficult. Until I do enough studies to understand how fast or slow things decay in that particular area of the forest, I can only hazard a guess."

"Okay. *Hazard,*" said Jack, barely concealing his impatience. "I really need you to give this case some speed, Shaw. I need some sort of time frame."

Shaw sighed. "Three, possibly four months. We got lucky, somewhat. The freezing temperature played a part in preventing too much decay, but the animals feasting on the remains mitigated the luck, somewhat."

"Have you determined how she died?"

Shaw shook his head. "Too early to verify, but my initial suspicion is that poison is the main culprit."

"Poison? Someone deliberately poisoned the child?"

"Deliberate? I'm not certain." Again, Shaw shook his head while examining the teeth of the dead girl, pointing at tiny, darkened stains. "This is possibly lead poisoning. Lead is a highly toxic substance. After being ingested, it enters the bloodstream and is absorbed and stored in many tissues and organs in the body, including the liver, kidneys, brain, teeth and bones. Children under the age of seven are especially vulnerable to lead's detrimental health effects, and often fall into a coma. Some suffer quite considerably before dying."

Grimacing, Jack asked, "When will you know for certain?"

"The lab has a few more tests to conduct. Hopefully, I'll know this time tomorrow—Thursday at the latest."

"The bone and feather?" said Jack. "You still haven't told me if either matches."

The consequence of a yes would be devastating. Had Adrian stumbled on to something sinister? Did the abductor of the little girl discover Adrian in the forest, hiding? Jack tried to calm his heart, hoped his face wasn't revealing his terrible, nightmarish thoughts.

"No . . . nothing yet," said Shaw, no emotion in his voice, a conditioned response—a response a little too quick for Jack's liking. "In the meantime, go home, Calvert. It's late. Get some well-earned sleep. You need your mind to be clear and sharp. As soon as I get something conclusive, you'll be the first to know."

Arriving home, Jack picked up the Wednesday evening newspaper in the hall and carried it into the living room. He made a cup of coffee and then sat down to read.

BODY FOUND. YOUNG NANCY?

Remains of a body were discovered in the desolate area of Barton's

Forest. The Belfast Telegraph *has learned that the bones are almost certainly those of Nancy McTier, granddaughter of the respected local doctor. . . .*

There were three pictures of Nancy, each showing a smiling, happy girl. The story detailed the grisly find, concentrating on the fact that the bones were discovered by ex-detective Jack Calvert, the man whose own son was missing.

Did he detect a question in the spirit of the story, speculating on the morbid coincidence? Was he becoming paranoid?

DOES TRAGEDY STALK THIS FALLEN HERO?

The bottom of the page gave a brief history of Jack, stating how he had been one of the most highly decorated detectives in the history of the police department.

Colleagues called him a cop's cop, one who instilled confidence, totally fearless. 'You felt safe when Jack Calvert was covering your back,' stated one police officer who wished to remain anonymous. 'The hierarchy got rid of him because he wouldn't take any s*** from them,' claimed another unnamed officer. But others saw him as a maverick, bending the rules to suit his own agenda, culminating in the controversial killing of a notorious drug dealer. The inevitable early retirement followed immediately. Not too long after that, his wife, Linda, was killed in a tragic car accident involving a drunken driver.

He couldn't care less what they said about him, but bringing Linda's death into the story filled him with anger. He kept having visions of traffic lights, blood oozing from the red, spilling on to the narrow and notoriously dangerous road, making it slick. He could hear the horrible sound of brakes no longer working, needing oil, red oil, and could see himself watching helpless as Linda went through the windscreen, her seatbelt dangling there, unused and useless like an unopened parachute rocketing towards earth.

No matter how close you get to it, sometimes the distance can't help but grow, thought Jack bitterly. Sitting back in his chair, he fixed his gaze on the ceiling. A chill was quickly seeping into the house, so he decided to light a fire. It would give him something to do, if only for a few minutes.

Just as he struck the large safety match, a moth fluttered in from the darkness of the window, and flew through the flame, dropping to the ground with wings turning to glowing ash. He didn't believe in omens, but it unnerved him—the moth's inexplicable appearance. It was unusual for moths to be seen this close to winter's end.

As he swept its charred body away with a tiny hearth brush, the phone rang on the private line, making his heart jump slightly. Dropping the brush, he quickly grappled with the phone, his nerves causing it to slip clumsily from his fingers.

"Adrian?" *Please God . . .*

For a few seconds, the only sound from the other end was a hollow seashell sound. Then a voice spoke.

"Isn't it ironic, don't you think?" The voice was soft, androgynous.

"What? Who is—?"

"To be able to rescue the dead, but not the living."

"Who is this? What do you want?"

"You're not a hero. You're a coward. We both know that, don't we?"

"What is it you—?"

"*Don't we?*" An edge was on the voice.

"Yes." Fumbling quickly in the drawer, Jack searched for his tape recorder. He couldn't find the bastard.

"It takes a special type of coward to leave his dying wife

mangled in metal while he slithers away, like a snake, to safety. Doesn't it?"

Jack's heart went to his throat. The room was moving, like a boat being swayed by waves.

"You . . . you have my son, Adrian. Don't you? Please . . . please don't harm him. I'll do whatever you want. Money? Is it money?"

"*Doesn't it?*" hissed the voice.

"Yes."

"A special type of coward?"

"A special type of coward."

"You're just like all the rest. A hypocrite. All crocodile tears for poor little innocent Nancy. But what about all the other poor little innocent victims? Eh? No one gave a fuck about them, did they?"

"What other victims? Who—?" The phone went dead.

Jack stood, motionless, the phone smirking at him, pulsating in his hand.

Think. Get the call traced. But his brain refused to shift into gear. Simple things became complicated. He could barely move, let alone think. The room was swaying faster. He feared that Adrian was dead, abandoned by a worthless father who could find dead strangers, but not him.

Call Benson.

Jack knew that Benson was not a great cop, one who would be remembered. He did everything well, but nothing exceptionally. Yet, he had a single-minded determination that always saw him reach the end of any task he initiated. But the leakage to the newspaper had left a bad taste in Jack's mouth and he knew that he would have to be careful of any information given to his ex-partner.

The phone rang again. He stared at it, frozen, almost fearful of its demanding sound. It rang again, seemingly louder this time, taunting.

Grabbing it on the fourth ring, he shouted, "What is it you want?"

"Jack? Are you okay?"

"What? Harry? Sorry . . . I—"

"Listen. I want to tell you one thing first. You can think all you want, that I'm not doing all I can to find Adrian. That's your prerogative. Even Anne thinks I'm not doing enough and she is giving me fucking hell over it. But I am doing everything possible, legal and illegal. The least people I involve, the less chance they have of getting into shit if it hits the fan. Understand?"

Jack was shocked at the emotion in Benson's voice. He was entirely grateful for it, also.

"Harry, I've been a bastard to everyone. My head is all fucked up at the moment."

"You haven't been a bastard; you've been a father, and a damn good one into the bargain."

Jack sucked in a gulp of air hoping to fend off the emotion caused by Benson's words.

"Jack? You still there?"

"Yes . . . yes, Harry. I'm still here."

"Some news. Don't know how significant it is, but could be something."

Jack's stomach tightened. "What is it?"

"We have a possible suspect for the little girl. And get this: he's a local barber."

Chapter Twenty-Seven

"There are horrors beyond horrors, and this was one of those . . ."
H.P. Lovecraft, *The Shunned House*

ARRIVING AT THE isolated cottage, shortly before ten, Jack proceeded to the front door. Heavy night rain was visiting, transforming the area into a mucky quagmire. A wire mesh fence surrounded the property, with a black iron gate punctuated by up-pointing bars with sharp tips.

A forensic team was gathering up numerous items for tagging, before placing them in plastic bags and containers. One of the bags contained parts of clothing.

The cottage had the musty smell of a place shut up too long. Lights were on, neutralising the dullness caused by the closed curtains.

Benson waved at Jack from a far room. He had a penetrating look on his face. Jack always appreciated that particular look of Benson's. It reminded him of a bloodhound, finally getting a sniff of its quarry.

"Officially, you aren't here. Understand? Wilson would have my balls in a sling." Benson handed him a pair of latex gloves.

"Of course," replied Jack, fingering the gloves, genuinely

appreciative, knowing that his ex-partner was sticking his neck out for him—again. He had debated with himself whether or not to tell Benson about the phone call. Reluctantly, he had decided that it was best to keep it to himself—at least for now.

"We got ourselves a real sicko," said Benson, indicating with a nod a pile of magazines scattered on the floor of the bedroom. "Look at this fucking shit."

From the seemingly endless collection, Jack lifted a magazine at random. The cover of the magazine was nondescript and innocuous, but when he opened it, its hideous contents were revealed.

Having glanced quickly at the first few graphic pages, Jack allowed the magazine to fall from his hands.

"Fucking child porn," said Benson, opening cupboards and drawers, his back to Jack. "The place is coming down with it. We discovered some clothing—a little girl's—hidden beneath the bed in the other room. Ominously, there were patches of dried blood on parts of the clothing. We'll have to wait until Shaw gets working on it, see if he can tie them in with the remains you discovered. It doesn't look good. We also found significant amounts of marijuana. By the looks of things, he's gone through more grass than a ladybird's arse."

While Benson rummaged for the sinister, Jack concentrated on the normality of the room, searching for the mundane, taking in every detail, feeling for omitted parts, trying to avoid the most common mistake of getting to the end of the puzzle, just to find a piece missing.

Was this the place of a paedophile, a taker of children? Of course, there was no such thing as a *place of a paedophile*. Their dwellings were as mundane and ordinary as themselves. In fact, this was their strength—their complete ordinariness, their chameleon-like ability to fit into any surroundings, any community. The image of a salivating loner was a dangerous myth created by the media to scare and sell. Granted, some of them did operate alone and were cunningly intelligent, but most were just everyday people, from all walks of life and associated with every profession, be it clergy, medical or judiciary. Even police officers.

Dotted about the walls were a few old wedding photos depicting the usual smiling groom and bride, surrounded by well-wishers and family. Another photo depicted the bride in white, from head to toe—a ghostly apparition in contrast to the charcoal grey of the groom. Two other people were in the photo. The best man and bridesmaid? The man had a patch covering one eye, but the woman was shying away, her gloved hand covering most of her face, leaving only the upper half to be scrutinised. The photograph stopped where the tip of the nose began. It was the eyes of the woman—not the patched eye of the man—that drew Jack in. The eyes had an animal intensity to them, as if they did not belong to the face.

Gardening was the theme in other photos: a woman—the bride, older now?—holding a silver cup and a plant proudly adorned with a winner's rosette. Others were of two men, standing outside a barber's shop. They were shaking hands, smiling for the camera. At least, one of them was smiling; the other—the one with the patch over his eye—looked quite dour. The men appeared eager, as if dreams were finally about to become a reality. In the background, attached to the shop's window was a sign, proudly proclaiming: Grand Opening. "A Fine Trim". A Cut Above the Rest.

Benson's finger tapped the photo, breaking Jack's thoughts "That's the bastard."

"What's his name?"

"Harris. Joe Harris. He's a local barber—though not the barber I go to," added Benson, quickly.

"How did he come to your attention?"

Benson removed a box from beneath a table. "Hey presto!" He turned the box on its side, allowing its contents to spill freely on to the top of the table. "The sweet, the one with the barber-pole wrapping. Your magical sweet, Sherlock—which, as I told you before, you shouldn't have touched: fucking with evidence." Benson captured one of the sweets and unwrapped its swirling coat, before popping the sugary rock in his mouth. "I have to admit that these are fucking good. Try one?"

Jack shook his head.

"What guided you to this place, Harry?" asked Jack, impatience lining his forehead. This evening's eerie phone call was still echoing in his head. He wanted to scream at Benson.

"Did you know that we have over one hundred and twenty barbers and hairdressers within a five-mile radius?" asked Benson, dislodging particles of the fragmented sweet from between his teeth.

"I do now." Jack rolled on the balls of his feet, hoping Benson's radar would pick up on his annoyance. It failed.

"We must have the most manicured inhabitants for miles," smirked the burly detective, before returning to the subject. "Luckily for us, a few still live in that bygone era of customer care. Only about ten still hand out sweets and little toys to their younger clientele. Better still, the sweet was not manufactured in any factory."

"Oh?"

"Nope. Our missing paedo fiend, Harris, and his late wife, Katrina, made these." Benson held a sweet between his finger and thumb. "A secret ingredient. Harris even designed the wrappers for them. What a guy."

"How do you know all this? Did you receive a tip-off?"

Benson tapped the photo again. "A process of elimination. We finally got to shop nine on our list, "A Fine Trim"—a fine mess, more likely. His boss, Jeremiah Grazier—the one with the Long John Silver patch—told us that Harris hadn't appeared for work in weeks. I was going to say this picture doesn't do Grazier justice, but as they say, 'What can't speak, can't lie.' It was Grazier who told us how Harris's late wife made the sweets just for the shop. Isn't that nice?"

"He didn't report it, or find it strange, his friend not showing up for work?" asked Jack, ignoring Benson's flippancy.

"Apparently not. Harris has done this sort of thing before, according to Grazier, so it was nothing unusual."

"What else did Grazier say?"

"Harris is a compulsive gambler and a bit of a drinker. No, let me rephrase that. Harris is an alcoholic. He drinks during the day to steady his hands when working. Fuck, can you imagine him giving you a shave? Anyway, Grazier hinted that Harris had been doing a lot of borrowing from loan sharks lately. He always seemed to be strapped for money, to cover the horses and dogs—probably flies going up the wall, as well."

"Have you spoken at length with Grazier?"

"No. Not yet. Didn't know we were walking into this sort of shit." Benson nodded at the magazines.

"I want to be there when you question him."

"What? Have you gone off the rail? I can't have you in the interrogation room!"

"Not the interrogation room. The observation room is fine."

"If Wilson even sniffed that I had permitted you to—"

"Wilson couldn't sniff his arse unless someone stuck his nose in it."

"And that's where you're becoming a right pain. You know, you've been in the station more often now, since your retirement, than you ever were while on duty."

"Nostalgia. I miss the old place. What time should I be there at?"

Resigned, Benson said: "Tomorrow at three. The barber's shop doesn't normally close early on Thursdays, but Mister Grazier said he would make an exception, said it would be a pleasure to tell us everything we need to know."

"Very accommodating of him."

"Well, he's obviously an accommodating sort of person." Benson smirked, tossing a large black Bible on the table. "I guess our Mister Harris is a bit confused as to which way he swings."

Opening the book, Jack glanced at the inscription. *To my friend, Joseph. May the Lord be perpetually at your side.* It was signed *Jeremiah.*

"I take it this is from Grazier?" asked Jack, showing Benson the dedication.

"More than likely. Apparently Long John Silver went door to door, selling these things, years ago. Probably had a parrot on his fucking shoulder."

"Where exactly does Grazier live?"

Removing a notepad from an overstuffed pocket, Benson flipped a few pages before scanning his illegible writing code. "He and his wife, Judith, own a large parcel of land, near the Cave Hill."

"Cave Hill?"

"Yes. That wilderness area over near Barton's Forest. Why? What's that look for? What are you thinking?"

"Nothing," said Jack, wondering if it was something.

Chapter Twenty-Eight

"Be near me when my light is low,
When the blood creeps, and the nerves prick . . ."
Alfred Lord Tennyson, "In Memoriam"

"WHAT WILL I say to them if they ask me if I ever suspected that Joe . . . loved children?" asked Jeremiah for the
tenth time in two hours. He sat on a chair, squirming uncomfortably, as if a tack had been placed on it.

"Tell them the truth," said Judith, placing her hands on his
shoulders. Immediately, he stopped fidgeting.

"What? What do you mean?"

"*Did* you ever suspect?"

"What? No . . ."

"Just tell the truth—when the truth is needed. Understand?"

"I'm confused. I'm afraid of saying the wrong thing, making
them suspicious of us."

"You won't. They will try and trick you, but you're too smart
for them. Be humble. Keep most—but not all—of your answers
short. Shrewdness shall be your fortress."

"I wish you could be there. I would feel a lot better."

"That would arouse suspicion in them. Why, they would
ask, would a grown man want his wife to accompany him to the
police station? Don't you see?"

He nodded. "Of course. But—"

"Moreover, you know I don't like people staring at me. They regard me as a freak."

"Don't. Don't ever say that. It breaks my heart to hear you talk like that." Jeremiah stood and faced Judith. "You are beautiful. You will always be beautiful. If they can't see your beauty, then let them burn in hell."

For the first time that day, a smile appeared on Judith's face. But the smile had an edge to it: it was the kind of smile where the mouth lengthens but the eyes remain fixed and hard.

"I've been neglecting you lately," she whispered in a low tone, close to his ear, awakening that tingling sensation between his legs. "I have a lot to make up for. Soon, we will be on our own again. You would like that, wouldn't you, just the two of us?"

He gently kissed her hand. "More than anything."

"Good. Now listen carefully. I will tell you what to say—exactly."

Chapter Twenty-Nine

"It is doubly pleasing to trick the trickster."
Jean de la Fontaine, *Fables,* Book 2

JACK STUDIED JEREMIAH via the two-way mirror, noting how the barber had placed his hands perfectly atop the table, his back straight and stiff. There was little doubt that the patch added a sinister look to the poor man's appearance. Good job Jack never judged a book by its cover—unlike Benson. The burly detective already had himself convinced of Grazier's wrongdoing—perhaps not in this particular case, but no doubt in other things that would eventually emerge.

"You only have to look at him," quipped Benson, prior to entering the room. "He looks like somebody from *Treasure Island* or Doctor Hook's Medicine fucking Show. I don't know if he's guilty, but he damn well should be, looking like that."

Benson had an infallible belief that over twenty years of being a cop had provided him with an insight into people's thoughts and state of mind—that by simply looking at the way the pupil of the eye changed when you asked the owner a question, you could determine guilt: *It's all in the eyes. Fuck polygraphs. They can be manipulated. But the pupils? Ha! You can't fuck with the pupils. Ever watch how a cat's eyes become so dilated when it spies on birds? That cat is thinking of how that little feathered pie will taste in its mouth.*

"First things first, Mister Grazier. I want to thank you for coming in on such a cold Thursday afternoon," said Benson.

"Anything to help the police, Detective . . ."

"Benson," said Benson, removing his coat as if preparing for battle, his huge chest straining on the shirt. "Just for the record, Mister Grazier, why did you not notify the police about Mister Harris's absence?"

"I thought Joe, perhaps, was on a drinking binge. He'd been having difficulties lately. It's not unusual for him to disappear for weeks—or sometimes months—on end."

"What kind of difficulties?"

"Drinking. Money . . ."

"Money?"

"He was doing an awful lot of gambling—more than he would normally do." Jeremiah took a sip of water. "He likes the horses and always knows a man who knows a man who has something or other on the highest authority. Unfortunately, their tips weren't tops. I think there were people . . . interested in him."

"*Interested?*"

Jack smiled at the expression on Benson's face.

"He owed money to people," explained Jeremiah.

"I see." Benson scribbled something down on a pad. "Do you know these *people?*"

"No; Joe did not divulge that information."

"Best of friends, and he didn't *divulge?* Didn't you find that strange?"

Jeremiah shook his head. "He probably didn't want me to get involved. I think they were loan sharks and such like-minded and dangerous people."

Removing a cigarette from its enclosure, Benson offered one to Jeremiah.

"No, thank you. I don't smoke—can't tolerate the smell. Don't drink either."

Undeterred and being an intolerant person himself, Benson removed a lighter from his pocket and struck the wheel a number of times before a tiny flame finally appeared.

"When I read about the evils of drinking and smoking, I gave up reading," Benson smiled wickedly, snapping the lighter shut, seemingly pleased that Jeremiah jumped slightly.

"Has Mister Harris ever borrowed money from you, Mister Grazier?"

Jeremiah nodded. "A few times."

"But this time he decided to go for loan sharks and other *like-minded* and *dangerous* people?"

"Apparently so," replied Jeremiah.

"Why do you think that is?"

"I told Joe that I could no longer encourage his habit, and that I would cease lending him any more money." Jeremiah shook his head. "I wish I had, now. I feel that in some way . . . I feel that I may have contributed to Joe's absence."

Jack noticed a little nervous tic below Jeremiah's eye patch; how it twitched slightly each time he spoke. He wondered if this was an indication of annoyance at the way Benson was directing the questioning, or simply irritation caused by the leather against his skin? Or something else, something entirely different but relevant?

"You said he had a problem with drink. How so?" Benson glanced about for an ashtray. Finding none, he flicked the ash on the floor, close to Jeremiah's shining leather shoes.

"Ever since Katrina, his much-loved wife, passed away, Joe

has been drinking excessively. More so than usual. Over the last few months, he had become quite irritable, not himself, even becoming agitated and angry with customers. A couple of times, I had to let him go home early, as his behaviour was becoming increasingly detrimental to the shop's image."

"Have you any idea what may have sparked this *behaviour?*" Benson tilted his head slightly. He seemed to be studying the leather patch adorning the face opposite.

"I . . . no . . ."

Sensing a potential withdrawal, Benson changed direction. "Look, Mister Grazier, I'm all for the sanctity of friendship, but there are times when not *divulging* information can get you into a whole lot of trouble. Trust me on this." Benson appeared to glance at the two-way mirror—much to Jack's chagrin. "What do you think—*intuitively*—may have contributed to Mister Harris's irrational behaviour?"

Bringing the water to his lips, Jeremiah took a good long sip. "Intuitively? Hmm. Well, I . . . we . . . we had police officers visit us, last week, asking questions about . . . about that little girl who went missing, a few years ago. Just routine questions, mind you, the same ones being asked of all the businesses in the area, I'm sure. But . . . I don't know . . . it just seemed to upset Joe, once the officers had left. I think he was upset that someone could harm the little girl. He seemed to be obsessed with her."

Jack could see Benson's left eyebrow move slightly as the large man's bulk moved somewhat towards Grazier.

"Did Mister Harris know Nancy McTier?"

"Nancy McTier? Oh! The little girl? To be totally honest, I don't know."

"Did you know her?"

"Me?"

"Had you seen her about, in the street, running errands, skipping—that sort of thing?"

"No."

Benson scribbled on the pad. "Did Mister Harris say anything to you after the officers had departed? Please take your time, Mister Grazier. It could be very important, what you tell us next." Benson's voice was a whisper.

Jeremiah nodded. He seemed to be studying a missing fragment of paint on the wall directly behind Benson's massive shoulders.

"He went straight to the first-aid cabinet—he has a little bottle of whiskey concealed there—and almost finished the bottle in one gulp. Then he said a profanity."

"Pardon?" Benson's face wrinkled into a puzzled look.

"He . . ." Jeremiah took another sip of water. "He said the 'f' word."

"The f word?"

"He said, 'Oh f.'"

"You mean fuck, Mister Grazier? He said, 'Oh fuck'?"

Jeremiah's face reddened. "Yes . . . that's exactly what he said."

Benson scribbled hurriedly on to the pad before diverting the conversation.

"You cut children's hair. Is that correct?"

Jeremiah half nodded. "Adults get their hair cut, as well, in the shop—not just children."

"Turns apiece, or did Mister Harris tend mostly to the children?"

"I . . . well . . . Joe mostly took care of the children. I have to admit that I don't have a great deal of patience with young people. Must be getting cranky in my old age." Jeremiah attempted a weak smile. Benson didn't acknowledge it. "Joe knew . . . Joe knew their football teams, the latest music trends. He was . . . *is* good at that sort of thing. I think the younger clientele felt more comfortable with him, I have to admit."

"Did he know them all by name?"

"Name? Oh, yes. I suppose. Knew most of their birthdays, that sort of thing. Always had a toy or a card with a few coins in it ready for the lucky child. He is very thoughtful that way."

"Is he indeed?" Benson glanced at the two-way, before continuing. "What was Harris in prison for?"

"What?" Jeremiah seemed taken aback by the curve of the questioning. "That was a very long time ago. I . . . I really can't remember."

Smiling like a fox with its mouth on the chicken's neck, Benson produced a slip of paper from a folder. "No? Let me refresh your memory, Mister Grazier. Does indecent exposure conjure up any memories?"

"Indecent . . . ? Oh! But that was when he was at college. A prank. He did a bit of streaking. Everyone was at it those days."

"Were they indeed? You also?"

"Me? No, certainly not," replied Jeremiah, looking slightly miffed. "No, it wasn't something . . . I didn't do that sort of thing. Joe thought streaking hilarious."

"Mrs Wilma McKenna, 26 King's Court, mustn't have had a sense of humour, *in those days*. She almost died when Flasher Harris swung his fishing rod at her window, the tiddler dangling from it."

Jeremiah said nothing.

On a roll, Benson continued. "Did you and Mister Harris do much socialising?"

"Socialising?"

"Go out for a drink, a meal, perhaps?"

Shaking his head, Jeremiah said, "No, I don't drink. I told you that already. And I rarely saw Joe outside of business hours."

"Where did he go to have a drink—that's if he went out, of course, and didn't have the medicine cabinet strapped to his back?"

Jeremiah seemed to be pondering the question. "I think the bar was called 'The Bunch of Grapes', though I'm not certain about that. We never really discussed his problem."

"I see," said Benson, scribbling on the pad. "Talking about *problems;* does Mister Harris have any other *problems* that you are aware of?"

"What kind of *other* problems?"

"Anything. Women, say. Does he have any girlfriends—someone we could call? Perhaps he's staying with a woman, as we speak?"

"No, Joe hasn't any girlfriends—at least none that I'm aware of. He mostly likes being on his own. After Katrina died he seemed to . . ."

"Seemed to . . .?"

Jeremiah took another sip of water. "He sort of lost interest in women."

Benson scribbled on the pad and, without looking up, said to Jeremiah, quite casually, "Did Mister Harris have an interest in children?"

"What?"

"Did he ever take any of the children out to the local McDonald's, places like that?"

"I really don't know. What kind of question is that? What's this all about? Why do you want to know if he took children to McDonald's?" Then, as if a great revelation had entered his head, Jeremiah looked shocked. "No! You think . . . you think Joe had something to do with that little girl's disappearance, just because I said about him acting strangely when the officers came to the shop? No, that's not possible. You're deliberately trying to put words into my mouth. What I meant to say was that he was probably agitated to think something had happened to her. He always suspected someone from that flea-pit of a boarding house just opposite us. You're deliberately taking my meaning—"

"Please calm down, Mister Grazier. I'm simply making sure that we have covered everything. I don't want to be calling on you again, interrupting your work."

Jeremiah closed his eyes slowly, before opening them. He appeared to become slightly agitated. "You're trying to make him a scapegoat, aren't you?"

Benson stood, his great size covering the seated Jeremiah in shadow.

"Coffee, Mister Grazier?" asked Benson, turning his back, walking towards the coffee-pot in the corner.

"No . . . no, thank you."

Jack almost missed it, the sleight of hand, as Jeremiah moved—almost imperceptibly—like a shadow on a wall. His long, bony fingers stretched just enough to touch Benson's writing pad. They did not move the pad, simply rested upon it, like a tarantula waiting for its prey.

"Would it be possible to go to the bathroom? All this water I've been drinking . . ." Jeremiah looked sheepishly at Benson.

"Yeah, I'm not surprised. You must have a bladder the size of a fridge. Go straight out the door, turn left, then second on your right. You can't miss the smell. Some dirty bastard usually leaves a large turd floating in there."

Waiting until Jeremiah had left the room, Benson made his way to the two-way mirror.

"Well? What do you reckon? Is he shitting himself, or what?" Benson grinned while continuing the one-way conversation at the two-way.

Jack sat on the toilet, waiting. He felt unclean, sneaky. The door opened and he knew immediately that it had to be Jeremiah, having rushed a few seconds ahead of him. He listened, like a pervert, as Jeremiah unzipped himself then began a soliloquy.

"Take a deep breath. Easy . . . Judith is with you . . ."

Jack listened intently to Jeremiah trying desperately to control his breathing. For the next few seconds, ramblings uttered from Jeremiah's mouth. Then nothing. Not a sound. No piss hitting the urinal, not even a fart.

Abruptly, the silence was broken by the sound of a zip snaking closed, followed by tap water running. The hand dryer gushed out its hot spurt of air and, a few seconds later, the door opened and closed, leaving a telling tranquillity.

Moving quickly, Jack hoped to get back before Benson started the interrogation. He opened the toilet door, clumsily banging into Jeremiah, almost tumbling over him.

"Oh, sorry about that," mumbled Jack, cursing his stupidly at believing Jeremiah had already left.

"That . . . that's okay," said Jeremiah, looking slightly rattled.

"Did you get a load off your mind?" asked a grinning Benson as Jeremiah walked through the door of the interrogation room. To Benson's delight, Jeremiah looked shaken.

Seemingly mortified, Jeremiah ignored the remark. The sudden and odd appearance of the man in the toilet had frightened him. A few seconds later, he re-seated himself, before clearing his throat with a cough. "I know you're only doing your duty,

Detective Benson, and I apologise for my outburst earlier. It's just such a preposterous idea. Joe wouldn't hurt a fly. Really. He's a very kind-hearted person."

Benson sipped the tepid coffee. It must have tasted bitter. He made a face just as the last sentence crawled from Jeremiah's mouth.

"Sometimes, Mister Grazier, we never really know what hides beneath the surface of skin and bones—all that complicated machinery. All it takes is for one of the wires to shake loose, disrupt the entire process of the delicate engine."

"I've known Joe most of my life. He is not a bad person."

"Knowing a person doesn't make him good, Mister Grazier. Didn't God know Lucifer for quite a while, the best of buddies at one time? Then old Luc had to spoil everything by growing a tail and fucking horns."

There was a noticeable shift in Jeremiah's body. His face tightened.

"I don't much care for your words, Detective Benson."

Rolling up the sleeves of his shirt, Benson exposed massive arms that had put the fear of god into numerous suspects, over the years. Looking every part the fearsome pugilist he had once been, he placed his pork-chop hands inches from Jeremiah's. He could have been a butcher, weighing up the best possible way to slaughter a nervous beast.

"I get a lot of complaints like that, Mister Grazier. My wife has told me the exact same thing."

Jeremiah stiffened, but no words left his mouth.

For the next few minutes, Benson flipped the pages of his notepad, checking his notes. Occasionally, he looked at Jeremiah, and smiled.

Jeremiah did not smile back.

"You've been a great help to us, Mister Grazier. I want to thank you for your time. You can go now."

Looking slightly relieved, Jeremiah stood and eased himself away from the table. Calmer now, he asked: "You *will* do your best to locate Joe, let him know that things are not always as dark as they seem? Of that, I'm entirely certain."

"Oh, don't you worry, Mister Grazier. We are going to do our damnedest to locate your friend. Of that, *I'm* entirely certain."

"Well? What did you make of him?" asked Benson, entering the observation room.

Jack shrugged. "Hard to determine from here. He seemed a bit nervous, but then most people are—especially when coming into contact with a big ape, like you."

"He's lucky we don't hang people on looks," laughed Benson.

"He read your notes," replied Jack, his voice soft.

The grin on Benson's face struggled. "What? What the hell are you talking about?"

"When you had your back to him, he read your notes."

The grin returned to Benson's face. "That time I made the coffee?"

Jack nodded.

"Well, sorry to disappoint you, but that was deliberate—a little trap I hoped he'd fall for. But he didn't. I kept him within my peripheral. He never moved once, smart arse."

Jack sighed. "He didn't need to. He read everything with his fingers."

Benson burst out laughing. "His fingers? Sure it wasn't his arse?" He laughed louder. "Jack, I think you need some rest. If I were you, I'd—"

"Tactile perception."

Benson shrugged his shoulders. "Tactile . . .?"

"Tactile perception. Blind or semi-blind people have the ability. That's how they read Braille. When the area of the skin is brought into contact with the line of Braille being read, it has a critical relation to the efficiency with which the tactile information is passed to their brain."

"Bullshit. What makes you such an expert on this quack theory?"

"It's not quackery; it's a scientific fact. I know so much about it because my mother was legally blind. She could read better with her fingers than I could with my eyes."

Benson looked slightly annoyed and indignant. "You never told me your mother was legally blind."

"The trained and practised fingers of a blind or semi-blind reader skim the symmetrical patterns indented on the paper, transferring to his or her conscious mind words, thoughts, ideas and emotions. The cognitive processes involved in reading scribbled writing and Braille are essentially the same."

"You're beginning to sound like that bastard Shaw, with all those fancy phrases. I'm still not wholly convinced."

"If you don't believe me, run the tape," challenged Jack.

"Okay. I will, smart arse."

Jack watched as Benson set the apparatus up.

"I could have been an actor, you know," said Benson, watching the screen flicker to life. "When I was younger, I almost went for it. Had the talent."

"Not the looks, though," said Jack, as he watched Benson on the screen turn towards the coffee machine. Benson was right, thought Jack: he *was* watching Jeremiah from his peripheral.

"Satisfied? Not a thing. Didn't I tell you that?" insisted Benson.

With a flick of a button on the remote control, Jack froze the picture. "There. See it?" Jack pressed the button again, and the story continued.

Benson's face almost clung to the screen. "I didn't see a thing."

Jack pressed the rewind button. Two seconds later, he pressed stop, then play.

"Watch his fingers. Nothing else," instructed Jack.

The same scene passed before Benson's eyes. "Fingers? I don't see no fucking movement from his—" Benson blinked. "Hold on. Go back. Hit the replay button again."

Jack pressed the button.

It *was* true. The fingers—or at least the knuckles had moved slightly. The rest of Jeremiah's body hadn't moved a fraction, as if he had become an ice sculpture.

"Hit it again," said Benson, his voice softer, uncertain.

There it was. The movement, slightly eerie, like a ghost walking on a grave.

"Fuck!" Benson shuddered involuntarily. Taking the remote from Jack, he played the scene over and over again, mesmerised. "That is fucking creepy."

"The greater the skin contact with the written line, the larger the tactile view," explained Jack. "Plus it was nice and warm in the interrogation room. Cold fingers do not make for good reading."

"Thanks for that belated information. Had I known old slippery tits was going to do a Liberace on me, I would have done the interrogation in the fucking fridge."

"You didn't mention about the material discovered at Harris's home?"

"Of course not. I wanted to see if Grazier could add some

interesting ingredients into that particular cake, without my mentioning it. The less he—and everyone else—knows about all this at the minute, the better. According to bank statements found in Harris's bedroom, he withdrew a large amount of money from his bank account. Ten thousand. Probably his life savings—when he wasn't donating it to *like-minded* people. I suppose he always moaned he didn't have a bucket to piss in, a good sob story when asking for money—oh, I almost forgot: he was issued with a passport, just over two years ago, but we couldn't locate it."

"Everything is pointing to Harris fleeing the country."

"What we have to figure out is: did he flee because of loan sharks or because he thought we were getting too close to him?" said Benson, removing a cigarette from a box along with a lighter, before offering one to Jack.

"Thanks."

Rolling the wheel of the lighter, Benson got no response. "Damn flint must be dull—a bit like my head, at the moment."

Searching in his pocket, Jack produced a box of matches.

"Do you think he knew?" inquired Benson, taking a light.

"About?"

"Harris's lust for children. Surely, he must have suspected something, that not everything was kosher with his best friend?"

"Perhaps."

"Do you think Grazier helped him to flee?" asked Benson.

"Flee?" replied Jack, squashing the cig on to the floor before opening the door to leave. "Time will tell if that is too generous a word to use."

Chapter Thirty

*"Still as he fled, his eye was backward cast
As if his fear still followed him behind."*
Edmund Spenser, *The Faerie Queen*

"YOU DID WELL. Stop judging yourself so harshly," said Judith, standing by the window, watching Jeremiah's and her own reflection in it. Rain was beginning to fall, melting against the glass.

"This afternoon was horrible in the police station. I kept having a feeling that someone else was watching me, someone a lot more dangerous than the big oafish beast."

"Oh, someone *was* watching you. Make no mistake about that. Those mirrors aren't put in for cosmetic reasons."

"The big cop kept asking about Joe. This troubled me, but I was clever and remained cordial, never angry. I gave him no hint of my building fury, for that would have provided him with ammunition against me, made him suspect something."

Rain was hitting harder against the window now, distorting Judith's reflection. She could no longer see Jeremiah.

"You'll be called back," said Judith, matter-of-factly.

Jeremiah's body jerked upwards, as if electricity had been connected to his seat, bolts of electricity tunnelling up his arse.

"Back? But I told them everything—exactly what you told me to say. Surely they think Joe simply fled, got out of the country as quickly as possible? What else could they think?"

Alternatives, you idiot, she wanted to say. *Lots for them to choose from.*

Judith studied Jeremiah, his agitated movements. She wanted to hurt him, physically, but he had grown to enjoy hurt—almost as much as she enjoyed administering it. She would have to devise other, more subtle, ways to bring the pain.

"You're not listening to me," said Jeremiah, his damp skin reflecting like plastic. "You said we would be alone soon. When are we getting rid of him? We've had him for too long. It's dangerous."

"Come here," she whispered.

Obediently, Jeremiah stood, before walking slowing towards her.

"Do I detect jealousy?" she teased. "A man jealous of a boy?"

"You promised we would be alone again, the way it used to be. Please . . . make him leave, go away forever into the darkness."

Judith smiled. It made her lips swell obscenely, like fat skinless snails.

"You would like that, wouldn't you?"

Jeremiah nodded reluctantly, as if he didn't trust the words lodging in his mouth, as if released they would turn him into a sobbing, mumbling wreck.

"The boy has told me that he loves me," said Judith, her eyes turning the colour of spilt ink. She could feel Jeremiah's entire body stiffen as she placed her hand against his chest, feeling the heart banging furiously against it, seeking freedom. It felt like a frantic bird, trapped in a bony cage.

Gently placing her nose against his skin, she inhaled, smelling his odour, his nervousness and insecurity mixing with a slight touch of post-interrogation fear. The smell was potent and intoxicating and she had to admit it was making her slightly dizzy—dizzy like the anticipation of heroin coursing through her body. But she was pursuing other smells trapped in the grease of Jeremiah's skin: smells of coffee, cigarettes and cheap aftershave. She could picture the big cop, standing there full of intimidation, towering over Jeremiah like a skyscraper of muscle and sinew. But it was the other smell she was chasing, the smell from the other cop, no doubt obscured behind the two-way mirror, studying Jeremiah.

Closing her eyes, Judith allowed her flared nostrils to come close to Jeremiah's skin, hovering lightly over the texture. She stopped, just above his left cheekbone, her heart jumping slightly. It was there, the smell of the other cop, the watcher. There were other smells as well: urine, dull excrement and cheap soap. Why was that?

"Did you ask to go to the toilet during the questioning?"

The unseemly question bothered Jeremiah. His body stiffened further.

"I . . . yes. I needed time to think. I didn't relieve myself. I only wanted time to get a small break from the—"

"That was stupid—and dangerous. You should never have left the interrogation room. It gave the look of avoidance. Why do you always prefer weakness over strength?"

"What was wrong with—?"

"*Sshhhhh,*" she hissed, her eyes slightly glazed. The smell was bothering her. Above all the shit, piss and cheap soap, she could detect the watcher. Had he followed Jeremiah into the toilet, suspecting something? What was it? She had smelt it before, the watcher's smell, but where? A distilled version, perhaps, but no doubt the same. Where? *Where?*

Angrily, she pushed Jeremiah away. "You're useless. You couldn't even carry their smells on your pathetic skin."

"What have I done that you're so angry? Didn't I do all that you asked? What's wrong? Help me to rectify it. Please. You know I'll do anything for you."

Swiftly regaining her composure, Judith whispered, "They are coming, coming after us. They will get here, eventually, like a gathering storm—make no mistake about that."

"What?" said Jeremiah, the blood draining from his exhausted face. "No, no, you're mistaken. I fooled them. I can fool them again."

"Fooled yourself. Not them."

"I . . . I will not allow harm to come to you," replied Jeremiah, his voice unusually strong.

She gently touched his head, reassuringly, her lips deflating into thin sharp lines.

"I know you won't."

Chapter Thirty-One

"For doubt and secrecy are the lure of lures,
and no new horror can be more terrible
than the daily torture of the commonplace."
H.P. Lovecraft, *Ex Oblivione*

IT HAD BEEN a rough and long day for Benson, and he wasn't looking forward to getting home. Anne would be waiting, asking had he found Adrian, making him feel as if he were somehow responsible for their godson's disappearance. It was a no-win situation. The story of his life. After this afternoon's less-than-successful interrogation of Grazier, he felt he had somehow let himself down in front of Jack, allowing the creepy barber to fool him.

Exhausted, he opened the door of his car, only to be confronted by a shadowy figure sitting in the driver's seat.

"You bastard! You scared the shit out of me. What the hell are you doing, lurking in my car, in the middle of the fucking night?"

"Did you check out Grazier's statement, the one he made to the investigating team?" asked Jack.

"Yes, I did—except he never made one, according to Starsky and fucking Hutch, two pimply-faced, just-off-the-tit, so-called detectives."

"What?"

"They said they took hundreds of statement that week. They meant to go back to the shop because our good friend, Grazier, wasn't there at the time, just pervy Harris."

"They didn't go back?" said Jack.

"Of course not. Starsky and fucking Hutch had more important things to do, like watching *The Simpsons,* the two wankers." Benson sighed, sounding disgusted. "I tell you, Jack, the sooner I get out of this business, the better. All these new recruits do *everything* according to the book. The problem is that when the book doesn't have an answer, they turn into fucking robots, unable to think for themselves."

"So, Mister Grazer misled us?"

"Misled sounds too nice. The weird bastard lied through his stinking teeth. I'll have to bring him back in again, and hit him with a few forget-me-nots, if you get my meaning," relied Benson, punching the palm of his hand with his fist.

"Best to let him stew," advised Jack. "He's intelligent enough. I'm sure he knows it's only a matter of time before we discover his lie. Hopefully, it'll make him do something careless, something to our advantage."

Benson smiled warily. "Why do I have a cringing feeling in my balls that you have an ulterior reason, other than Grazier, for hiding in my car in the dead of night?"

"Thought it best to ask you, face to face," said Jack. "You probably would have hung up on me, had I phoned. I need a favour."

Upon hearing those words, Benson groaned. "A favour? That usually means breaking the law, as far as you're concerned. What is it this time? You want to break into the main computer at headquarters? Steal Wilson's lunch? C'mon, enlighten me as to your next adventure."

Despite his own weariness, Jack couldn't resist a tired smile. "I need you to let me into the old Graham building."

Relief crept on to Benson's face. "You hide in my car like an assassin, just to ask me for a grand tour of the Graham building? Strange—earlier today, Wilson released a memo stating that the investigation into the corpse found in the orphanage was now completed, and that no more man-hours were to be wasted on it."

"That was a quick and thorough investigation," said Jack, disgusted. "Another unsolved murder quickly cooked for the books, swept under the carpet."

"Dead homeless people don't vote, you understand?" Benson grinned. "Anyway, I don't see a problem with letting you in for an hour or so. How does tomorrow morning, early, sound?"

"Tonight."

"Tonight? Like now, in the fucking dark? There's no electricity in that place. Surely it can wait until the morning?"

Jack eased over to the passenger seat. "I've torches in the back of my car, two streets away." He patted the driver's seat. "Besides, sometimes the dark can be more revealing than the light."

"What a fucking dump," said Benson, pulling up at the main gate of the Graham building. "Shitty looking during the day, but at night it looks even more fucked up. Are you sure you can't wait until the morning?"

But Jack was already exiting the car, his torch smearing the darkness with its chalky beam. A large chain coiled itself tightly against the ornate gates, laughingly preventing intruders from entering. A lock, the size of an apple, was intertwined with the chain. It looked impressive, the security—though not to Jack.

"I know," quipped Benson, as if reading Jack's thoughts. "All you have to do is go to the back wall and fall through to the fucking basement, just like Charlie Stanton."

Benson removed a key from his pocket, and, within seconds, the coil of chain fell to the ground, noisily.

"Do you mind telling me what this is all about?" asked Benson as both men walked up the winding, dilapidated path leading to the front entrance.

"In all honesty, Harry? Nothing. Perhaps I'm just clutching at straws. I've covered ever single place where Adrian could be, and when I heard that the homeless man was trying to find shelter in this godforsaken place, well . . ."

They entered through the hall of the building, the torches' powerful beams guiding them.

"Careful," advised Benson. "The place is riddled with woodworm. I almost went through one of the fucking floors, yesterday. Scared the shit out of myself. And that was with plenty of light."

In the breathing darkness, the sprawling nature of the empty building came together in a rush, like two hands cupping. The building reeked of rotten cabbage. The pong was overpowering, with a constant curious stench, like a sprawling slum district under threat of a deluge of open sewage.

"This is where old Charlie found the praying fruit," announced Benson, as they entered the one-time laundry room. "Forensics did their usual stellar job of finding sweet fuck all. Though to be fair to that lazy bunch of bastards, I've a sneaking suspicion that Citizen Charlie went through any clothing in the room, destroying and stealing what he could. He didn't strike me as an upstanding member of the community, old Charlie."

"You shouldn't assume the victim was gay," said Jack, trying not to allow Benson's homophobia to irritate him.

"A big fucking dildo up his arse and he wasn't a fruit? What was he doing, then? Clearing the wax from his ears?"

Exiting the laundry room, they turned left, into the main dormitory. It was completely bare of all contents, with the exception of tiny piles of excrement camped throughout the enormous room.

"Nice, eh? The biggest shit hole in town," smirked Benson. "Who said homeless people weren't house-trained? What a fucking stench."

Despondency was seeping into Jack as each room revealed nothing. The old building was deeply depressing. He had witnessed the inside of prisons more homely than this and wondered what it had been like for the children forced to reside here.

"Had enough of the magical mystery tour?" asked Benson. "If we stay any longer, it'll be daylight, and you really don't want to see this place in all its glory. Trust me on that."

"I just want to check out the last couple of rooms. Then that's the end of it. It was good to get it out of my system, Harry, even if we found nothing."

Benson nodded, and removed a cigarette and lighter from his pocket.

"Want one?" offered Benson.

"No, not right now. I want to check the rooms out first."

"You don't mind if I stop for a smoke? I'll catch up with you in a few minutes." Benson rolled the lighter's wheel. It failed to spark. "I don't believe this shit."

"Here," Jack handed him a box of matches. "Keep them."

Proceeding down the corridor, Jack turned left into a large room, the words "Control Room" stencilled above the entrance. Like every other room, it was practically bare, as if swarms of human locusts had ascended, stripping it of everything but a few withered posters and pages attached to the walls, and an old rusted bed frame securely bolted to the floor.

A wry smile appeared on Jack's face. "They'll steal everything unless it's bolted down."

"Control Room keys must *never* be carried outside the Control Room" stated one of the dusty pages. "Failure in this regard will result in disciplinary action."

Someone had scribbled something directly beneath the order. Jack could make out the words "fuck off" and "wanker", but the rest of the rebellious wording was illegible.

Directing the beam of light over the rest of the walls, Jack concentrated it on scribbles of handwriting, hoping to recognise the writing or perhaps a coded message. A couple of times, the beam faded, and he cursed himself for not having checked the batteries in his haste to get to this monstrosity of a building.

"Don't go dead on me, now," he whispered, just as the batteries did just that. "Damn it!" The room was plunged into a choking darkness and, for some inexplicable reason, Jack suddenly felt vulnerable, like a child lost in a haunted house.

Quickly stabbing his hand into his pockets, he frantically searched for his matches, before remembering.

"Harry!" he shouted, feeling puerile, disorientated. "*Harry!*"

"What?" responded Benson's echoing voice. "What the fuck is it now?"

"Light! I need some light! Battery is dead!"

Even from the distance, Jack could hear Benson mumbling about not even being able to have a smoke in peace.

"Where are you?" shouted Benson, walking down the corridor. "Which fucking room?"

"The control room! Near the very end of the corridor." Jack's voice quietened as he heard Benson's footsteps nearing;

saw the beam from his friend's torch slice through the darkness.

Suddenly, tiny beams of light oozed through the wall, ghostly, like the eyes of dead creatures, landing on Jack's waist, forming a slithering belt, before disappearing into the night.

"Harry? Harry! I'm in here, next door, in the control room. There's a sign above the door."

"Okay, okay, I hear you; but it's impossible to see any signs," mumbled Benson, defensively. A few seconds later, he appeared at the door of the control room. "Have you finished playing hide and fucking seek? Can we go now?"

"I want you to go back in, next door, and shine the torch against the wall, just like you did a moment ago."

"Have you lost it? If you think for one minute that I am going back in there, just to shine the—"

"Stop the moaning, and do as I ask," hissed Jack, his voice bringing a heavy silence to the room.

Benson glared at his ex-partner before reluctantly complying. "This had better be fucking good, Jack. I've had enough of this shit."

A few seconds later, Jack could hear Benson stomp his way through the adjacent room like a big kid newly chastised by a parent.

Nothing. The control room sat in total darkness. Jack wondered if he had been hallucinating, all the strain and fatigue taking their toll.

Defeated, he shouted in to Benson that it was okay, to forget about it. "It was nothing, Harry, just my tired eyes playing tricks."

Benson muffled a reply. "I haven't been able to turn the damned torch on. Didn't you check the batteries in these—hold on . . . there! It's back on! Any luck?"

"Hold it right there, Harry! Hold it right there!" Light was seeping through the wall, like an old movie projector, dust motes dancing on the beams.

Tracing the light, Jack pressed his fingers against the entrance holes, feeling them fitting perfectly against his skin.

"Can you see my fingers, Harry?"

"Of course I can fucking see them. What the hell are you playing at?"

"Don't move that light. I'm coming in."

Moving quickly and as carefully as possible, Jack groped the walls for direction, all the way into the next room.

"What's this all about?" asked Benson.

"Could be nothing—could be a million things," replied Jack. "Scan the light along the wall, just where those holes are."

Benson ran the beam along the wall, slowly, as if removing paint. There were ten holes, in all.

"Okay. The wall has holes. So what? So have I," said Benson, flippantly.

"Those holes aren't accidental," said Jack. "Too evenly distributed, too elaborate." Brushing his hand along the floor, removing grime and dust, Jack slowly revealed what the years had tried to hide. "Scuff marks . . . harsh imprints. Probably from chairs."

Benson shrugged his shoulders. "And?"

"Give me your torch. Look through any of those holes. I'm going next door. Tell me what you see."

Seconds later, Benson watched the light from the torch reveal the one item of interest to Jack: the bed.

"I still don't get it," mumbled Benson, just as Jack made an appearance back in the room.

"Voyeurs."

"Peeping fucking Toms?" said Benson, spitting out the dust from his mouth. "Are you sure? How can you be certain?"

Jack's face was bleached white. Even in the smothering darkness, Benson could see that quite clearly. More worrying to Benson was Jack's lack of response. His ex-partner had said nothing; and in saying nothing, he said everything.

Chapter Thirty-Two

"The City is of Night; perchance of Death,
But certainly of Night."
James Thomson, *The City of Dreadful Night*

OPENING THE FRONT door of his house, an exhausted Jack almost walked on the small package resting on the carpet in the hall.

His name was typed on the front, but no address. He wondered why anyone would drop it through the letterbox so late at night.

Opening it, he was somewhat puzzled to discover a pair of laced panties, black in colour, moderate in size and expensive to the feel.

"Who on earth would send . . .?" A photograph fell from the panties, landing beside his feet. "Sarah . . .?" The photo was of a smiling Sarah, posing adjacent to a painting in the gallery.

Glancing at his watch, Jack decided to call her. It was then that the thought struck him: she was still in Dublin, and wasn't due back until tomorrow. Perhaps she had simply cut her trip short?

He lifted the receiver and dialled her home, but all he got was her answering machine. Undeterred, he decided to call the hotel in Dublin. "Hello, would it be possible to put me through to Sarah Bryant, please?"

A few seconds later, Sarah's groggy voice answered.

"Hello?"

"Sarah? Jack. Sorry. Did I disturb you? Were you sleeping?"

"Jack . . .? No, I mean yes, but not to worry, darling. What's wrong?"

"I know this sounds strange, but did you send me something tonight, wrapped up in a brown package? Got someone to deliver it?"

He could hear her body shift in the bed. She seemed to be getting herself more comfortable.

"Something? What kind of something?"

A cold sensation was beginning to stir in Jack's stomach. The hairs on the back of his neck moved.

"A pair of lace panties."

"*What?* Are you serious?" She laughed. "No, of course not. Why would I do such a thing? I mean, I know I'm a bit of a—"

"Sarah, are you sure? I need you to tell me if it's a little gag you're pulling on me? There's a photo with them. It's you, standing next to a painting of what looks like a large orange tree with seagulls nesting."

There was an iron silence from the other end before Sarah spoke. "*Doves.* Not seagulls. *Peace in the Orange Grove,* by Paul Thornton. He's a young artist with a bright future. How . . . I don't understand? That photo is in my bedroom, in a drawer."

The cold sensation had turned to ice in Jack's stomach.

"It's probably nothing, just one of your employees messing about, trying to wind us both up." Jack knew that his reasoning sounded feeble, but there was little he could say to clear up the mystery.

"Should I leave, head home, Jack? I'm due back early tomorrow morning anyway. I can cut my stay short."

"No, don't do that. There would be little point to it. As I said, it's probably nothing."

"Okay . . . Jack?"

"Yes?"

"Have you heard anything from Adrian?"

"Not yet."

"I'm really sorry about what happened, when he walked in on us. That was my fault. All I had to do was phone, instead of showing up at your door like that."

"It had nothing to do with you," he lied. "We'll get him back. Don't worry. Now, I want you to get some rest. See you tomorrow. Make sure you phone me as soon as you get back from Dublin. Okay?"

"Yes. Goodnight, darling," said Sarah and the phone went dead.

The visit tonight to the orphanage had unsettled him, physically as well as mentally. He had hoped to get some well-earned rest, as soon as he arrived home, but the mysterious package had put an end to that.

No sooner had he turned to leave the room than the phone screamed. Quickly, he picked up the receiver.

"Sarah?"

Heavy breathing competed with static and dull sounds. "Did you like your little present?"

Jack gently squeezed the button of the tape recorder. He was prepared this time.

"What have you done with my son?"

"You're wasting valuable time, *ex*-detective Calvert, just like I wasted valuable time waiting for your whore of a girlfriend in her bedroom tonight. You're such a hypocrite, pretending to be worrying about your son, pretending to be searching for him. You're more concerned about fucking the whore, aren't you?"

Jack squeezed the phone until the knuckles in his hand looked ready for popping. Trying desperately to control his voice, he said, "I love my son more than anything on this—"

"*Liar!*" hissed the voice. "Such a liar. You tell me one more lie and the phone goes dead—as will your son."

Breathe easy, he told himself. *Good long gulps.*

"What . . . what is it you want from me?"

Snide laughter. "I waited two whole days in that whore's house, just to give her a surprise. But she failed to show. Is she there with you now, fondling your balls, kissing your cock?"

"No, she isn't here. She wasn't here."

"You're not lying to me? I don't like to be lied to."

"No, I am not lying. I haven't seen Sarah in days. I thought that was her on the phone, when I picked it up."

"Did you now? So sorry to disappoint." More snide laughter. "I'm sure Adrian would love to hear how you're out fucking instead of searching, you hypocritical bastard."

A damned noise was banging in his head, making it difficult to hear the tormenting voice clearly. It was the sound of his heart, bang-bang-banging, in his chest.

"Please . . . please don't hurt him. Why are you doing this to him? He's just a child. He didn't do anything—"

"Please don't hurt him," mimicked the voice. "No? Why? You've already done that, over and over again, haven't you?"

Jack's mouth turned arid. He didn't reply.

"Haven't you?"

"Yes."

"And you want to rectify that, don't you?"

He did not reply.

"Don't you?"

"Of course."

"What would you do to have Adrian back?"

Jack tried to swallow. "Anything. I'd do anything. Is it money you want? I can get you—"

"I have a little proposition to make. I need you to kill Sarah Bryant," said the voice, calmly, as if reading a recipe from a list.

"What on earth are—?"

"Shhhh. No interruptions. Pay attention. Time is running out for us all—especially for your son, if you don't comply." The voice waited, and, getting no response, said, "Good. That's more like it. Now, you will use your police skills to kill her—you're good at that. I will leave the method entirely in your hands." Laughter. "But it must be painful. She must suffer before she dies. That is imperative. Do you understand?"

"I . . ."

"Do you understand?" hissed the voice.

"Yes."

"Good! Cheer up. To listen to your unenthusiastic voice, one would think it was Adrian you're being asked to kill, not some deserving whore. Now, to help you become more *enthusiastic,* I will award you points for imaginative techniques used. You need to achieve twenty points—no, make that twenty-one, my favourite number—to free Adrian. The more points you accumulate, the quicker he goes free. Should you fail to reach the designated number—say, within a week—well, I'll leave that to your imagination."

The phone went dead.

"Hello? Hello!" shouted Jack, before quickly regaining his

composure. He hit a button and asked the voice at the other end, "Did you get it?"

A few seconds of silence. "No, sir . . . a few more seconds," said the young police officer's voice. "That's all we needed to trace—"

Despondent, Jack slammed the receiver back into its cradle, cracking it.

Chapter Thirty-Three

"The truth is rarely pure, and never simple."
Oscar Wilde, *The Importance of Being Earnest*

"SARAH TOLD ME that she can't think of anyone who would wish to harm her," said Jack, replaying last night's tape recording for Benson. "She doesn't recognise the voice on the tape, either."

"That's a great help. So informative." Benson smirked, sipping a cup of coffee at Jack's kitchen table. "What about a disgruntled artist? We all know how touchy you bastards are. Perhaps Sarah displaying your paintings in the gallery was taken as an affront, filling him with jealousy?"

"I doubt very much if someone would kidnap Adrian just because my paintings were exhibited."

Benson snorted. "I doubt very much if someone would break into a church and kill the vicar. But hey, guess what? It happened!"

"That was a robbery and vandalism. Didn't the report say money was stolen and a couple of statues smashed up, and that the vicar had stumbled upon the intruders by accident?"

"A doctored report. We don't know what—if anything—was taken. Wilson leaked the robbery scenario to his friends in the press. Probably thinks people will feel more secure believing it was simply a robbery gone wrong, rather than some devil worshipper running about, chopping the heads off statues."

"Chopping the heads off . . .?" Deep furrows appeared in Jack's forehead. "How was the vicar murdered? Any idea, or has that been doctored as well?"

Benson shrugged his shoulders. "Initial reports say he was beaten with a blunt instrument. A rock of some sort, more than likely. Why? What's that look for?"

"I'm just thinking about that headless corpse at the Graham building."

"Well, you can stop thinking about it. That case is firmly closed. That's Wilson's orders. So don't even think that you are going back in there. You're not. Now, why don't you take my advice and get some sleep? You're no use to Adrian if you look and think like a zombie."

"I'd appreciate if you'd keep me informed of any developments," said Jack.

"I would've appreciated you informing me sooner about the phone calls," replied Benson, staring at Jack.

"I know. I should have."

"No more solo escapades. If you can't trust me, then you can't ask for help when it suits you." Rising, Benson removed his overcoat from the back of the chair, and squeezed into it.

"Fair enough. You'll be the first to know of any new developments."

Buttoning his overcoat, Benson looked at Jack. "I'm sorry about not being able to offer some protection for Sarah. Wilson would laugh me out of the office. Besides, I hate asking the bastard for anything. You'd think it was coming out of his miserable pocket, the way he's reacting."

"Don't worry about it. Besides, Sarah wouldn't have allowed it. She said I was paranoid, and that she was more than able to take care of herself."

"Ballsy kind of a woman. My favourite," said Benson, opening the front door before walking down the pathway, towards his car.

Closing the door, Jack returned to the kitchen to finish off his coffee. He wouldn't be seeing a bed any time soon. Too many questions; too many theories to speculate on: *stoned to death in the sanctuary of holy ground?*

It sounded almost biblical.

Chapter Thirty-Four

"Ask you what provocation I have had?
The strong antipathy of good and bad."
Alexander Pope, *Imitations of Horace*

"GOD, TONIGHT, SARAH!" shouted Jack, his composure long gone. "The stalker was in your very bedroom, less than two days ago. This isn't a game. You've got to let me get you some extra security. I've a couple of ex-cop friends who are more than willing to do a bit of guard duty. All you need to do is—"

"I insist that you stop causing a scene, Jack. My clients are not accustomed to loud noises in the gallery," hissed Sarah, politely smiling at the faces glancing in her direction. "You are going to have a massive heart attack, if you don't calm down."

Jack breathed deeper. "Okay. I've calmed down, but you can't avoid what I've just explained."

"Did you know that there have been over fifteen burglaries in the last two months alone, in my area?"

"This wasn't an attempted burglary, Sarah. He was in your house, in your bedroom, stalking it out."

Gently, calmly, Sarah placed her finger on his lips. "You're doing it again, the cop mentality, the paranoia. You're beginning to really piss me off. I am not one of your damsels in distress,

waiting for a knight in shining armour, Jack. I don't lead a shel-
tered life, despite the erroneous messages the opulence may be
sending you. For your information—and I know how cops just
love information—long before I met you, I had been threatened,
robbed, even had a knife held to my throat by a would-be rapist;
I've witnessed a client being shot dead on the streets of Tokyo,
and God alone knows how many obscene phone calls I've
received, not to mention drug dealers accosting me to buy their
dope. So, please, do not insult me with the macho bravado bullshit. It simply doesn't wash. I am more than able—and willing—
to protect myself. Now, when I remove my finger,
you—we—will not discuss this sad, pathetic creature, any further. You are insulting me, just by having this conversation.
There is this little thing in the air, slipping between us. Don't
allow it to destroy us, Jack."

Defeated, Jack wearily asked, "Well, at least allow me to stay
at your place, for the next few nights. Not for your sake—for
mine."

Immediately, Sarah laughed. "I like the sound of that. Me
protecting you. You'd make a good politician, Jack Calvert, if
such a thing as a good politician existed."

"Is that a yes?"

"It isn't a no. Give me some time to think about it. Now, if
you don't mind, I've a business to run." She kissed him quickly on the cheek, shooing him out the gallery door equally as
quickly.

In the hospital, Jack replayed the scene over and over again,
wondering what he could have done differently. The combination of all the warnings should have acquiesced into a whole that
made Sarah feel vulnerable. But they had not. The opposite had

happened—disastrously so. He was the one at fault. He should have had someone watching her at all times, protecting her, despite her protestations. Intuition was one of the strongest advantages he had—something he normally would never have ignored. But he *had* ignored it, and Sarah, not he, had paid for his complacency.

He couldn't hear the doctor's words, explaining the damage done by the perfectly honed dumdum bullets, only the sniggering voice on the phone, saying, *Did I catch you and her off guard? You really didn't believe I needed a pathetic bastard like you to kill the whore? Silly Mister Policeman . . .*

Chapter Thirty-Five

"Superior people never make long visits . . ."
Marianne Moore, *Silence*

IT WAS TIME to move on, thought Jeremiah, scanning the old newspaper. Judith had been correct—as usual. Time for the shop to close, for good. Besides, his heart was no longer in barbering. The place was losing customers at an alarming rate. Granted, having only one barber was a major factor—people had no patience, nowadays, wanting everything *now,* not in ten to fifteen minutes. But his own behaviour wasn't helping: the dropping of instruments and the wrong change placed in outstretched hands, his mumbling response to queries concerning Joe.

Jeremiah always suspected that customers liked Joe more than him, preferred his easygoing personality, the jokes he sometimes told, his up-to-the-minute news on sport and politics. Liked him until the rumours began to spread, saying that he had had something to do with the little McTier girl. Now, the shop was tainted, frequented by a few diehard customers, customers who assured Jeremiah that they did not believe the rumours. They knew Joe too well.

He knew that he shouldn't be thinking about Joe. But he

wasn't strong; not like Judith. He thought about Joe most days; knew he was destined for hell for what he had allowed to happen—and all because of the boy. Had he left him to freeze to death in the forest, perhaps things would have been different.

Judith had promised to get rid of him, but so far she hadn't kept her promise. She had always kept her promises, and this also he blamed on the boy. He was beginning to think that she was lying about her intentions—something she had never done before—and once again, he suspected that the boy was behind this.

It was all the fault of the boy. He was a Jonah, a millstone weighing them down. He was everywhere in Jeremiah's head. Even the newspapers—the sinful rags he had promised never to read—carried articles about him.

'Latest on murdered gallery owner', exclaimed Monday's miniature headline on page four. *"We've received some calls and some tips, but unfortunately we haven't had a significant development on Saturday night's shooting,"* said a spokesperson for the police.

Police believe robbery was the motive, but have not completely ruled out a disgruntled artist. Bizarrely, the one-time and highly decorated detective, Jack Calvert, has been named as a 'close friend' of Ms Bryant. Calvert's son, Adrian, disappeared in mysterious circumstances, almost two weeks ago . . .

Highly decorated detective. The three words made Jeremiah's stomach do strange little kicks.

He couldn't wait to close the shop. Once he got home, he would ask—*demand*—that Judith do something about the accursed boy. If she refused, well, he would have no choice other than to—

"Open for business?" asked a man's voice.

The voice spooked Jeremiah. He hadn't even heard the door jingle its alert.

"I . . . I was closing actually," mumbled Jeremiah, quickly crumpling the newspaper into the wastepaper basket.

"I'm sorry. It's just that I got an unexpected call this evening, from an old flame," said the man, easing his coat off, much to Jeremiah's obvious annoyance.

Before Jeremiah could object, the man sat down on the chair.

"Been years since I saw her," said the man, rubbing the stubble on his chin. "Want to look my best. Know what I mean?" The man winked at Jeremiah, annoying him further.

Defeated, Jeremiah began to whisk a tankard of soapy liquid, transforming it magically into foam, before transferring it to the man's skin.

Cut-throat razor in hand, he quickly attended to the soapy face, allowing the soap to settle but not congeal.

A good barber never allows soap to congeal was the first rule Grazier had learned, all those years ago, as an apprentice. *If it congeals, it closes the pores; the stubble becomes like nails.*

Whetting the razor, Jeremiah skimmed the thin strap of supple Russian leather until the metal gleamed. Expertly, holding the razor with thumb and three fingers, he made a swathe in the air with the lethal blade before commencing on the smooth and unproblematic areas of the man's face.

The customer looked vaguely familiar, but Jeremiah couldn't put a name to the face. Too tired even to try. Probably one of those morbid people who had heard about the shop, about Joe. Probably wanted to boast to his friends that he had been to *that* barber's shop.

With a slight, invisible movement, Jeremiah's razor removed

the peppered-black soap, leaving the man's left cheek gleaming reddish pink.

"That was terrible about that little girl, the one they found in the woods," said the man.

"What?"

"The little girl in the forest, a couple of days ago. Haven't you heard?" The man looked at himself in the mirror. "Terrible to think what monsters there are lurking in a nice town like this. I've always said that it's not the monsters under the bed we have to worry about, but the ones on top."

Jeremiah felt his hands shake. He willed them steady.

"I don't really want to discuss any of that, sir," said Jeremiah, his voice strangely soft. "It's an unsavoury topic for the town."

"Unfortunately, we have no death penalty here. Anyway, I suppose the death penalty is too merciful for a bastard like that," said the man, ignoring Jeremiah's words. "I would take the bastard out to the forest and—"

"I don't much care for your language, sir. I will have to ask you to refrain from swearing in my shop."

The man looked embarrassed. "Oh, I'm sorry. I didn't mean to swear. But every time I think of that cowardly bastard, picking on the weakest members of society, well . . . my blood just boils something shocking. Probably a weak individual, himself. Women and kids. Good at that. But you put him up against a man and he will shit his pants, every time. He was probably a bully at school, a torturer of dumb animals. I bet that's how he gets his *real* kicks, having sex with dogs." The man laughed out loud. It was a bawdy, backstreet laugh. It ground against Jeremiah's skull.

Gently, Jeremiah rested the razor on the pliable neck of the man, whose protruding Adam's apple was the size and shape of a sparrow's egg.

Just one slice, whispered a voice in Jeremiah's head, as his hands began to shake again. *That's all it would take, and loud-mouthed know-it-all will be gone into the night. You can do it. Show Judith you've got what it takes.*

The man stared at Jeremiah, his eyes now suddenly piercing. He seemed to be reading his mind. The eyes seemed to be daring him.

"Are you okay?" asked the man, breaking Jeremiah's thoughts.

"What? Yes . . . of course." With a slight curve of his elbow, Jeremiah removed all remaining stubble. "That's you, sir. Hope you're satisfied with the shave?"

Carefully examining his face, the man ran his hand over the smooth skin.

"Excellent job. I'll have to come here in future. My old place is being demolished, turned into a café, of all things."

"There's a lot of that happening everywhere," replied Jeremiah, accepting payment in one hand while the other quickly worked the door. "Have a good night, sir. Safe home."

"Thank you for the excellent shave. You'll be seeing more of me in the future. That's a promise," said Jack Calvert, heading into the night air.

PART TWO

SPRING:
NEW LIFE; OLD REVELATIONS

"When the hounds of spring are on winter's traces . . ."
Algernon Charles Swinburne, *Atalanta in Calydon*

Chapter Thirty-Six

"Where dead men meet . . ."
Samuel Butler, "Life After Death"

MEGAN THOMSON KNEW that she shouldn't have eaten the trout, freshly caught by her husband, Peter, at the rocky stream. Now she was paying the price, suffering from terrible bouts of diarrhoea, cramps stabbing into her gut like a hot bayonet.

"That damned fish you caught," she moaned. "I shouldn't have come on this trip."

"Stop all the complaining, will you? No one else has said a word about the fish. You simply didn't want to come with us. You made that plain enough last night, in the tent. Probably thinking of that pathetic loser, Kevin Hamilton."

Uncomfortable, the other two members of the camping trip looked away from the quarrelling couple.

"You really are making a fool of yourself in front of all your friends—*again.* I don't know what you're talking about. Just don't take your sexual inadequacies out on me," said Megan, feeling her stomach percolate. How long had he known about Kevin? She tried to keep her face impassive.

"When you finally kick the bucket, I'm getting you a

headstone that reads, 'Here Lies My Adulterous Wife—Cold as Ever!'" Peter smirked at his wit.

"Your headstone will read, 'Here Lies My Husband—Stiff At Last!' Now, get out of my way!" shouted Megan, pushing Peter to the side, her bowels on fire, as she headed quickly—for the fourth time in less than two hours—towards the privacy of trees just beyond the campsite.

"Make sure you're downwind," laughed Peter, watching her scurry for relief into the trees' shadows.

Just as Megan thought it couldn't possibly get any worse, it began to rain.

"Fuck! I don't believe this!"

As she moved further inwards, the rain quickened. She was far out in the forest now, and the trail leading back—the opening from which she had emerged—was no longer visible. She saw only a snarled wall of dark bushes and leafless, decaying trees.

"Far enough," she whispered, removing the wipes from the packaging, as she crouched down, feeling instant relief as the shit flew from her arse. The relief was tremendous.

The weak moon was slowly vanishing behind inky clouds, leaving her limned in its dying light, making her feel uneasy and vulnerable, her confidence ebbing. She had never felt this way before, in all her camping trips, but there was something in how the darkness had suddenly come upon her, like a living, breathing thing. It felt hostile.

Ten minutes later, she stood unsteadily, drained. "Never again," she vowed. "No more fish. No more fucked-up camping trips."

Moving cautiously, she edged out of the designated toilet area only to feel something squish beneath her feet, making her slip, tumble forward and scrape her face on thorny bushes.

"I don't believe this," she whispered, disgustedly. "I've slipped on my own—" Her voice slowly trailed off when something told her that it wasn't her own shit, but something else, something more sinister.

"What on earth . . .?" Everything around her seemed suddenly removed, hardly real, as she stared, zombie-like at the ground. Momentarily, she seemed to be robbed of all breath, as if under water, and felt pain beginning to swell her head. She tried to move, she tried to run, but there was a gap, a delay between the thoughts in her head and screams from her mouth. She began to dry heave.

"Help!" she screamed, over and over again, until her voice was nothing more than a croak. *"Help me . . ."*

The bodies rested side by side, pressed into the dirt, their exposed throats black with blood, their ribs resembling rusted radiators.

Chapter Thirty-Seven

"Prying curiosity means death."
H.P. Lovecraft, "The Rats in the Walls"

EASING FROM THE vehicle, Jack saw his reflection in the side mirror and he hesitated, held there by his own weary eyes. He looked dead. Six weeks of searching for Adrian had aged him terribly. He felt that at any moment a nervous breakdown could come crashing down upon him, leaving him a drooling fool trapped in dark memories. Worse, it would leave Adrian without hope, and that alone was the spur that forced him not to succumb.

In the encroaching dawn, he reluctantly stood, binoculars tight against his eyes, scanning the vastness of the Graziers' land, scouting for any additional messages. Unbeknownst to him, less than two miles east and more than four hours previously, Megan Thomson had become a discoverer of dead things.

In the distance, the remote farmhouse and surrounding area came into view. The building looked disjointed—a mirror fractured. The land was lumpy and the edges were contoured, girding the lone road leading to the large farmhouse. The road itself shone with the black, denuded glare of ageing asphalt, guiding the way like a liquorice tongue.

Unnaturally, the place was absent of the noise of machinery and human occupancy. Only the sounds of branches rubbing together, like stridulating crickets, could be heard; and the only movement came from a pageant of crows swooping in for landing in one of the haggard-looking fields where three scarecrows took centre stage, guarding.

Ignoring the ragged sentinels, the crows rummaged at will, drilling with their beaks.

The scarecrows' spectral strangeness absorbed Jack, making him think of an effigy of Calvary.

The Graziers' farmhouse clung, crab-like, to the side of a massive barn. Jack could make out rusted machinery poking from the barn's dilapidated siding. Everything seemed chaotic and unused as if no human hand had touched it for decades. Off the side of the road, he could see the bulky outline of an old car, a dent the size of a portable television blazoned along its side. The car rested in the shadow of the farmhouse, arrogantly or complacently exposed. There was little doubt in his mind that it was the same car that had come at him on a snowy night all those weeks ago, recklessly indifferent.

Through misty morning light and shadows to the last line of fields, Jack began to wend his way cautiously in the direction of the farmhouse, avoiding the carved path. The soil beneath his feet was slightly sodden and spongy. It stank with the smell of rainy green. Overhead, the sky was ugly and gorgeous, like a bloody salmon gutted to the neck.

Red sky in the morning, he thought, gently touching the gun housed inside its shoulder holster, reassuring himself.

He had no evidence of wrongdoing by Grazier—only raw belief; but more importantly, he had no right. Benson would explode if he knew what he was up to, compromising the case on *raw belief*. Wilson would have him arrested. That was a certainty.

He had to be careful, though. Search enough, but not too far. Find something—something sufficient to allow Benson to have a search warrant issued—then quickly get the hell away from this godforsaken place.

Hunkering down, he edged his way towards the Graziers' car, tumbling awkwardly beside it, feeling like an old fool acting out a stuntman manoeuvre.

The car sat crookedly, one tyre in a muddy hole. Running his hand over the dent, his eyes scanned the tiny particles of blue scratched alongside the original white. There was no doubt in his head that the blue was his own car's paint.

There was a single window halfway to the corner and he moved to that now, crawling on belly and elbows, crouching so low to the ground that his shadow hurrying along beside him looked deformed, misshapen.

Knackered, he rested his head directly below the windowsill.

Easy now . . . don't rush it . . . don't mess up at this stage of the game.

Allowing his left hand to crawl up over the warped windowsill, its decayed wood crumbling on the pads of his fingers, he could feel chunks of peeling paint, and knew instinctively at that terrible moment that they contained lead. If someone had ever placed them across the tongue of a little girl called Nancy, they would have caused her to go into convulsions and die—a terrible and excruciating death.

He could hear Shaw's gruff, acerbic tongue, mocking him, relegating him to a non-professional civilian: *Calvert, speculation is reincarnation. Neither can be established without proof, you fool.*

Proof? You want proof? I'm going to get you tons of the stuff; so much, in fact, that you'll not know what to do with it, you nasty old bastard.

Removing his gun from the shoulder holster, Jack checked it one last time, making sure the initial chamber was empty—a precautionary tactic in case of an accident—and then returned it to its warm bed of leather, before standing, upright, his back tight against the wall.

Leaning forward, he peeked inside the window. Too dark. Impossible to see a damned thing. His armpits were damp. He could smell his own body odour and something else. It wasn't pleasant. Not fear, he told himself. Caution.

Taking a deep breath, he moved stealthily towards the front of the farmhouse.

As expected, the large front door wasn't locked. Miles of rocky roads and forests isolated the Graziers, and a visitor would be an irregularity, an oddity. The Graziers certainly had no need for locked doors. Perhaps others did.

Manoeuvring steadily, Jack eased into the darkness of the hall, making a sharp right in the direction of a room. Falling into the room, he allowed his eyes to adjust to the dimness. It was a bedroom—of sorts—with a single bed stretched out in the centre. The bed was accompanied by a small chest of drawers, paradoxically making the room look even emptier. It was the barest room he had ever seen in his life.

Atop the chest of drawers were sealed hair tonics. Hair clippers sat alongside smirking cut-throats. There were a few magazines in the room, honeycombed into a wooden bracket against the wall. The magazines were mostly, not exclusively, back copies of *Barbers' Times.*

Jack scrutinised the inside of the chest of drawers, careful not to disturb the contents. Socks and underwear. A few shirts, white and heavily starched. Did Jeremiah wear those? Jack cast his mind back to his experience in the barber's shop, when he had thought that Grazier was going to cut his throat.

The room reeked of loneliness, though the unmade bed contradicted that. Could this be a visitor's bedroom, a fugitive's? Could this be Harris's bedroom?

Cautiously, Jack proceeded out of the room and down the thin hallway where the darkness was easing, a little at a time, to a uniform grey. Eventually, his surroundings brightened enough so that he was able to look about and take stock.

The other rooms in the house flowed easily into one another, devoid of any clutter or furniture. They were almost clinical, unlived in, like props for a stage. The furniture was neat and perfectly rendered, as if from a picture. The rooms disturbed him, though he couldn't say why—only that their ambience was tranquil, yet strangely menacing.

Stepping out of a room, Jack scanned the hallway. A closed door to his left beckoned. Beneath the door wrote a pencil of thin light, beckoning him towards it. He eased opened the door, revealing a bedroom far larger than the lonely specimen he perceived to be a visitor's. This room did not have a woman's touch, but Jack speculated that it belonged to Judith and Jeremiah, if only by a process of elimination.

He panned his eyes around the room and was automatically drawn to a lone picture adorning the wall. *Susanna and the Elders,* stated the inscription. It was a print of a painting by Artemisia Gentileschi, an artist familiar to Jack as one of the first women artists to have achieved recognition in the male-dominated world of post-Renaissance art. A fiend by the name of Tassi had raped her, and the trauma of the rape and subsequent so-called trial had impacted on Artemisia's life and paintings.

Her graphic depictions were cathartic and symbolic attempts to deal with the physical and psychological pain inflicted upon her by men.

Susanna and the Elders told the story of a virtuous young wife sexually harassed by the spying elders of her community, as she sat bathing; they had hoped to blackmail her into having sex with them. The painting depicted the gesture of one of the Elders raising his finger to his lips, warning Susanna to be silent, while the other Elder loomed large, leering menacingly and conspiratorially. The canvas spoke volumes with a single scene, and the finger to the lips was exceptionally chilling.

There were two wardrobes stationed on either side of the painting, guarding it. One had its doors slightly ajar, and he could see quite clearly its contents of plain-looking dresses. Above them, a rack of shoes—black, conservative—rested. They looked well used and scuffed—travelled, a more diplomatic word. The astringent smell of mothballs was overwhelming.

Easing the doors of the other wardrobe open, Jack scanned quickly, finding nothing of significance; he chastised himself for wasting time, being a voyeur. He needed something tangible, something to convince Benson of the necessity of a search warrant. Deep down, he was beginning to believe that he was clutching at straws. Whatever he was searching for wouldn't be here, waiting for him to find it. It would be well hidden.

It was a splinter of morning sun coming through the window that made him glance over his shoulder. The golden sliver reflected off a box perched on a shelf, catching his attention.

The circular box was quite beautiful, if somewhat macabre. The dark, mahogany lid depicted a decapitation scene. It was more of Gentileschi's work in the form of the beautiful, if somewhat ghoulish, *Judith Slaying Holofernes*.

Holding the box in his hands, Jack shook it gently, as if not wishing to disturb the contents. Something sounded from within.

For a heart-stopping moment, the bedroom door opened slightly. His body stiffened, but it was only the morning wind flexing its muscles. Nervy but undeterred, he spilt the contents of the box on to the bed.

Photos. Twelve. All Polaroid. Children. Naked. Different poses.

Jack shook his head. He wondered immediately what the implications were. He didn't want to find this sort of stuff, confirming his worst fears: Grazier and Harris were obviously working as a team.

But why would Grazier keep the pictures in his bedroom? Wouldn't his wife discover them? Was she in on it as well? Shit, he was unprepared for that. Up to now, he had assumed that paedophilia was exclusively an all-male disease—a perfectly reasonable assumption when he thought back to the people arrested while he was in the force.

There *had* to be a logical explanation. Perhaps Grazier and Harris had threatened her, forced her with threats?

The thought made him fear for Grazier's wife, almost as much as he feared for Adrian. Why was she not about? What had Grazier done to her? What if Harris hadn't fled the country, but was here, somewhere on the property, armed and lurking about?

Jack knew that, unlike the magazines found at Harris's cottage, there could be no turning up his nose at the photos. The clue to Adrian could be staring him in the face, at this very moment.

Deliberately forcing himself to enter clinical mode, Jack no longer allowed the pictures to be repulsive. If he allowed them to shock, then they—not he—would hold the power.

Turning to the task at hand, he studied the photos, trying desperately to find some clue as to their location or the perpetrator who introduced them to the world. He remembered once, down at the station, how they had enhanced a similar-type photo and got lucky when the taker of the snapshot was exposed in the fear-filled pupil of the child. But he doubted very much that luck would be with him on this case. So far, luck had avoided him. Besides, these pictures were grainy, not too professional looking. They were battered and finger-worn. Why was that? Paedophiles could update their collections at an alarming rate, via the Internet. So why hold on to these coarse items? Why were they so special that Grazier or Harris refused to dispose of them, and risked getting caught?

Initially, he had thought that perhaps one or two of the pictures would be of the McTier girl, but the more he studied the pictures, the more he understood their startling truth: they were all of the same child, a boy.

The face of the little boy was obscured by carefully placed shadows. The taker of the photographs didn't want the boy's entire face to be exposed. Why was that? Fear that the face would betray him, lead a trail right to his door, if the boy were recognised?

The boy was bony and awkward, with stunted chest and ribs that jutted out like plastic butterflies. But it was the tortured eyes that Jack kept returning to. They looked dead, impassive, but still betrayed something, something that went beyond terror and fear. There was power in the darkness of the pupils, unmerciful power. They seemed to be laughing at him, mocking, as if knowing the power they would one day wield. He had witnessed the eyes someplace else, but he couldn't recall, almost as if they had hypnotised him into not remembering.

Think. Where?

Debating whether to pocket the photos or return them to their wooden enclosure, Jack finally decided on the latter, placing the box back perfectly, resting it just where the barely visible dust ring left a halo on the shelf.

Time to leave, he told himself, retracing his steps down the hallway.

Stepping outside the farmhouse, he was immediately assaulted by the cold, refreshing his face. He felt terribly unclean, tainted by the photos. He was gasping for a cigarette, but resisted the urge. He would wait until he got back to his car. Now was the time to leave, alert Benson to what he had seen. He hoped that his ex-partner would have a good squad of cops here within the hour, depending on the rough terrain. A helicopter would get them here in less than ten minutes, but he doubted if Benson would try to get Wilson to authorise that.

Leaving this terrible place was the rational thing to do, but reasonable actions had become alien to Jack, lately. Instead, inexplicably, he made his way cautiously down the snaking path, directly towards the sheds. Some mysterious force was pulling him towards them.

Once again, the stillness of the place unnerved him slightly. Not even a crow cawing from the nearby fields. *Where are the Graziers?* He thought about taking the gun from its holster, but cautioned himself against such an act. Breaking and entering was bad enough. Openly armed into the bargain? He doubted very much if he could talk himself out of that one. Wilson would love that.

Where to start? he wondered, studying the large hangar-like sheds. There were so many of them. Most appeared dilapidated beyond repair. Only one seemed to be in a functional state. It was windowless and this piqued his curiosity.

Treading softly, he made his way towards the entrance of the shed and leaned an eye against the partially opened door. The stench oozing menacingly from the shed hit him full in the face, forcing him to pull away, take a breather.

C'mon. Move. It's only shit and blood. You've smelt worse than that. A million times worse than that.

By eliminating more and more possibilities, Jack's mind and body became more and more fearful of what waited on the other side of the door.

He took a deep breath. Entered . . .

Chapter Thirty-Eight

"'Will you walk into my parlour?' said the Spider to the Fly;
'Tis the prettiest little parlour, That ever you did spy . . .'"
Mary Howitt, "The Spider and the Fly"

THE SHED DOOR squeaked loudly and Jack cursed it as he
slithered in. A glow from an old paraffin heater painted
pale jaundice on the wooden walls. He considered the stifling
stench that was running riot. It tasted like garbage and discarded
meat. Gratefully, he welcomed the fumes from the heater
almost as if they were sweet-smelling perfume battling against
the combined army of stenches.

Other than the humming of an old freezer, there was little
sound in the shed. From the corner of his eye, a tiny red glow
faded in and out of the shadows and fractured light. It was like
an SOS signal. He turned to see its source, his eyes trying desperately to focus in the semi-darkness.

A woman, obscured, sat in shadows, almost motionless, a
cigarette trapped between her teeth. It unsettled him, her statue-like presence. She did not speak, simply stared disconcertingly at him while sucking gently on the cigarette. There was
little doubt in his mind that this was Grazier's wife, Judith. She
seemed to be appraising him in soundless speculation, and he
marvelled at the control she maintained as she spoke.

"This is private ground. You're an intruder. Trespassing can get you killed. I have the right to defend myself against intruders." Her voice was barely a whisper, but it was strong, a voice that made one listen. "What's your name, and what are you doing on my land?"

For a second, Jack's tongue became wood, refusing to acknowledge her questions. Fortunately, his brain was as sharp as ever. "Jack . . . Jack Benson. My car skidded off the road, about a mile back. I took the nearest path, hoping to find a phone box so that I could call the emergency breakdown company. I didn't mean to trespass, but I saw your farmhouse and banged on the door. There was no answer."

Jack heard a sound, not too far from where Judith sat. It was an eerie, unsettling sound, and it made the skin crawl on the back of his neck.

"Well, you've wasted your time. We don't have phones— don't have too many modern appliances. All the so-called towns around here are little dots," said Judith. "The nearest dot, Bellvue, is about two miles away. Your best bet would be backtracking until you come to Bellvue. Plenty of phones there, I believe."

"Two miles? To be honest, I'm just about beat. That accident winded me, bruised my ribs slightly. I noticed your car parked at the farmhouse. Would there be any chance of getting a ride into—"

"Car doesn't work. Hasn't worked in years. No, best thing would be for you to head to Bellvue, on foot. They'll take care of you. Good people there, I'm told."

That sound, again, coming from somewhere to her left. It was like a faint cry; like the muffled sound of a baby, as if someone was pressing a pillow on its face.

Jack's heart moved up a level.

"What's that sound? The little squealing sound?" he asked, forcing a smile, hoping she couldn't read his eyes, the hardness in them.

"Sound? Oh that. You really want to know?"

Noticing too late the cut-throat partially hidden and resting in her curled-up fingers, Jack quickly became conscious of his gun pressing against his body as he edged slightly closer, warily.

The squeals became louder, more numerous, as if permission had been granted by some strange command, as if they were warning him to flee, make a run for it while he could.

What seemed an eternity ended by Judith's movements as she reached to reveal the source of the horrible tiny sounds gnawing at his ears.

"Rabbits. Don't you just love them when they make that sound of complete hopelessness?" said Judith, effortlessly pulling a squealing rabbit unceremoniously by the ears from a large trap stationed at her side. The creature made the sound a hungry baby makes searching for a nipple—a haunting sound so ominous it reached to the ghetto of Jack's soul.

She held the struggling rabbit inches from his mesmerised face, its whiskers nervously capturing dust motes. Slightly twitching the blade, she slit the animal's throat, releasing a leaf of blood that covered her fingernails like rose petals.

Instinctively, Jack's hand moved to his throat while the rabbit jerked violently.

"Don't pay it no heed," advised Judith, watching Jack's eyes skim over the dead creature. "It's only a rabbit, a dirty, very ugly rabbit." She wiped the sweat from her face, leaving a trail of skidded blood on her mouth. The blood glazed her lips, making them fat and obscene, like garden slugs captured by the sun.

Jack felt himself grimacing and tried to undo his face, but she'd seen it. Only now, so close to her, was he able to take in his surroundings. There were rabbit skins everywhere, festooned upon the walls and resembling leaves of tobacco. They retained their tiny faces, each adorned with a grotesque, posthumous grin.

His intuition told him not to take his eyes off Judith—not while she held the cut-throat. He studied her, afraid to blink or look away in case she vanished. But she remained firmly corporeal, staring at him with an arrogant expression of ownership, letting him know that this was her territory and that he was the stranger, the intruder.

She stepped out from the shadows, and he saw that she was completely naked, with the exception of patches of wet rabbit blood desecrating parts of her skin. It shocked him, her blood-stained nakedness, but as she moved slightly to his right he wondered if this had been a deliberate strategy, to shock him, make him take his eyes off the evil-looking cut-throat, its silver edge grinning wickedly with fresh rabbit blood?

"Well, thank you for pointing out the nearest town. It's very much appreciated," said Jack, edging slowly backwards. "My apologies if I startled you. It was never my intention to—"

His mobile phone went off, buzzing in his pocket like angry wasps. Only when he reached for it, did his mistake hit home.

Bluffing his calmness, he spoke directly into the phone, wanting to crush it with his hands. "Hello?" he asked, forcing a smile, trying desperately to keep his voice calm.

"Jack? Where the hell are you?" asked Benson, his voice panicky. "I've been calling your home for the last hour. Listen, I've some news. It isn't good, Jack, I'm afraid."

A throb was beginning to germinate in Jack's skull. Ice fingers touched his stomach. He dreaded what was coming next from Benson's mouth.

"Yes, I'm listening." Where was Grazier's wife? He hadn't observed any movement from her, but she was gone.

"A group of campers, over near Barton's Forest, discovered the remains of two bodies."

Oh, dear God . . .

"Jack? Are you there, Jack?"

Jack's mouth had dried up like cotton balls. He was finding it difficult to produce saliva.

"Yes . . . yes, I'm still here." He could hear something—someone?—directly behind him. He felt the thickness of his gun, close to his ribs. It was reassuring. He listened to Benson while calculating his next move. *Where the hell is she?*

"There's no easy way to tell you this, Jack, but initial inspections from Shaw and the clothing indicate that the bones belong to males."

Jack felt dizzy. He couldn't breathe. Everything seemed to be spinning.

"Jack? Jack, you still there?"

Stop the self-pity. Be strong. Be very strong; otherwise you are going to die in this filthy, wooden cave. He willed his mouth to move. "Yes, John. I . . . I had a slight accident, but I shouldn't be *long, John*. I'm fine. I should be on the road, shortly."

"Jack? Who the fuck is John? This is Benson. Jack? What on earth are you mumbling about? Did you hear what I just said about the two bodies being discovered over at—?"

Jack snapped the phone shut and listened to its echo along the wooden walls. In his mind, he tried to picture the door behind him, how many steps to it? Slowly, he eased the phone into his pocket, his right hand navigating it, while the left touched the holster. Releasing the button on the leather lip, he felt the warmth of the gun as he eased it slightly out.

Without warning, Judith suddenly stepped from the shadows and came within touching distance of Jack. The speed of her movement mystified him as she brought a double-barrelled shotgun to his face, pushing it tight, nipping his skin, chilling it.

"I dare you to even blink," whispered Judith, pressing the gun tighter into his face.

Paradoxically, only when the muzzle was pressed further did the sensation of chillness disappear—his skin had warmed the steel. Now there was only a dull, invasive pain.

"What the hell is this all about?" said Jack, his fingers easing the gun from the holster.

One second. Just give me one second, prayed Jack, his index finger curling on the trigger of his gun.

"*Don't,*" she hissed. "Don't move a muscle. I wouldn't want your brains splattered all over my floor, mingling with the guts of the rabbits—not yet, anyway. Now, very slowly, remove your hand from your pocket. Nice and easy. That other cold metal feeling, on the back of your head—that's another double-barrelled shotgun. A sandwich, you could say, and you're the meat."

Jack didn't need to be told what it was. Three years ago, he had allowed himself to be exchanged for a hostage in a failed bank robbery. He still got shivers and the shits each time he thought of the two ugly holes pressed against his skull.

Judith searched Jack's pockets with one hand, finding both phone and gun. She tossed both items on to a bale of rags.

"Little phone has a big mouth. Exposed your lie, Mister . . . ?"

"I've already told you. The name is Benson. Jack Benson."

"The gun?"

"I'm a private investigator. I was hired to find a gang dealing in stolen credit cards. I was travelling, just like I said. I'm hoping to meet up with the local police to confirm some information sent my way. What's all this about? I've already apologised for being on your land. What else do you want me to—?"

"*Do not,* for your own sake, be condescending," hissed Judith, pressing the barrels tighter. "We wouldn't like it."

From the back, the other shotgun was pushed tighter against Jack's head. Jack pictured Grazier standing directly behind him, grinning, his fingers twitching nervously on the gun's double triggers, ready to pull them at the slightest movement.

"Now, for the last time, just who are you?" Judith's voice trailed off. A puzzled look imprinted itself on her forehead as she leaned closer, sniffing the air. Her skin reddened as the nostrils flared, capturing something intriguing. She parted her lips in a crooked smile, as if remembering something particularly nice—or nasty—and her face suddenly became a holy revelation. "You . . . you're the watcher."

Puzzled, Jack replied, honestly, "I don't know what you're taking about." He felt as if the shotgun at the back of his head was drilling its way through his skull, trying to find his brain. He tried not to think of the firing pin hitting home, sending an explosion into his head. He badly wanted the gun to be removed.

"When I was little, it was discovered that I possessed a gift, a sensitive olfactory gift," said Judith. "Do you know what the olfactory system is, Mister *Calvert?*"

Jack's lips barely moved but he couldn't help showing his surprise as her mouth revealed his name.

"I've already told you. My name is Benson. Jack Benson—"

Judith pulled the hammers back on the shotgun. The sickening sound ran up the rail of Jack's spine.

"One more lie, Mister Calvert, and you are dead. Now, I'll ask you again: do you know what the olfactory system is?"

Wearily, Jack said, "I wouldn't call myself an expert, but I know it concerns the sense of smell."

Judith looked as pleased as a Sunday-school teacher. "The olfactory is like a light bulb transmitting signals to the limbic system in the brain, where memory is used to recognise different odours. The limbic system is not only a memory storage area, but it also regulates mood and emotion. The average human's bulb is a forty-watt, fifty if they are above average. Can you guess what mine is, Mister Calvert?"

Jack shrugged his shoulders. "Fifty?" *Those eyes. What was it about her eyes? Where had he seen them before?*

"Eighty, Mister Calvert. Eighty." She reiterated the last word as if she had suddenly become Moses, climbing down from Mount Sinai, the Ten Commandments at her side. "At first, I didn't comprehend the power of my gift—although I suspect it wasn't nearly as developed in my youth as it is now." Her mouth formed a sardonic slit. "It's only lately I have begun to appreciate it more fully, using it to my full advantage."

The rabbits were squealing again. Eerily silent for the last ten minutes, they had suddenly become more audible, more numerous, as if they were communicating with each other. The sound was making Jack's skin crawl.

"When Jeremiah came back from the *interview*," continued Judith, "I detected a combination of smells clinging to his oily skin. One of the smells had bothered me so much that I found it difficult to sleep. Jeremiah had been no help at all in finding its ownership. No, it was left up to me, as usual, to figure it out, and once I had determined that smell, I knew where I had encountered it before."

She's delirious. Jack now fully understood that she was an addict, hooked on some powerful, mind-altering drug. Everything pointed to that: from the emaciated body to the dilated pupils; even down to the lethargic voice and rambling incoherence of her words.

"Puzzled, Mister Calvert? At first, I was puzzled also. Your smell was irritatingly baffling. I had tasted it somewhere else, but couldn't quite place it. Then I discovered it had been right under my very nose—literally. You carry the same smell as the beautiful boy at the lake, your son, Adrian," she said, calmly. "The same smell I can detect from you at this very moment."

Jack gritted his teeth, trying desperately to keep his voice calm. His heart was swelling with pressure.

"What do you know about my son? Where is he?"

"Know? I know *everything* about him. I know what you do not. I know what you could never imagine. I know his heart, his soul. More importantly, I know everything about *you,* Detective Calvert—or ex-detective, to be more precise. I know how you murdered an innocent man, leading to your *early retirement.*" Judith made a snorting sound. "Early retirement? A euphemism for being kicked out of the police force, disgraced."

Jack's eyes hardened slightly. "He wasn't innocent. He was a drug dealer, selling to kids. He deserved all he got for the lives he destroyed. Now, what do you know about my son?"

"Lots. His eyes were pond-blue like his father's, but set closer together and lacking the history only age and experience can bring. But here's a kicker. Want to hear it?"

Jack didn't reply.

"I know about your *wife,* how you murdered her, drunk as a *pig*—oink oink—at the wheel; how you covered it up, cowardly, like the hypocrite you and your ilk truly are."

An invisible fist slammed into Jack's stomach. His insides were a contradiction of heat and cold, competing against each other: hot shit, iced blood.

"You seem shocked. Why? Didn't I tell you that I knew Adrian's heart and soul, his tongue—that sweet-tasting piece of plum meat? He liked to use that, you know? A lot. And not just for talking, I should add." She smiled. "He hated you for what you did to his mother, for ignoring him for years with your silent abuse, putting job before son, for fucking that whore from the gallery. Adrian was the perfect candidate for an Oedipus complex, and you helped him to achieve it."

Inside, Jack was cringing, fully aware that she was speaking in the past tense each time she mentioned Adrian. "*Where* is my son? You can still get out of this with your life. Armed officers are heading in this direction, as we speak."

"Are they indeed? Good. They'll find a dead trespasser when they arrive. An armed trespasser into the bargain." She removed the shotgun from his face, leaving two perfectly circled marks indented on his skin. The menacing looking razor was quickly brought back into play, inches from his clammy face.

Jack was trying to think, but his brain was going into overdrive. Too many things happening at once. Her breasts were swelling, obscenely so. They looked weird, but he couldn't draw his eyes away from them, no matter how hard he tried.

"You like my breasts? So did Adrian." She smirked, pressing the razor against Jack's mouth, her lips touching his skin. He could feel air on his skin as her nostrils went to work, investigating. "If you only knew what your smell is telling me—all the apprehension and fear." She removed the razor from his mouth, calmly placing it on the tip of his nose. The smell of dried rabbit blood filled his nostrils. It stank like a corroded penny.

"Don't be foolish. You don't want to do something now, only to regret it—"

"*Quiet!* Did I grant you permission to speak—to *grunt?*" Her hand was trembling as she clenched her teeth, pressing the razor against Jack's nose, penetrating skin. "Sit yourself down—*slowly*. Don't do anything silly." She transferred the razor from Jack's bleeding nose to his throat. "You even sneeze and I'll pop your Adam's apple like a cork in a wine bottle."

Obediently, Jack sat down on a pile of rags, the other shotgun on the back of his skull following him.

"It's not you, or your husband, we're after. It's Harris. We know he killed the little McTier girl." If Jack believed that final revelation was going to make Judith panic, reveal all, he was very much mistaken.

"Harris?" said Judith, sniggering, her eyes darkening. "You know nothing. Absolutely nothing. Meeting people with identities other than your own can teach you all sorts of things, Mister Calvert. Did you not know that? The most valuable, obviously, is how to enjoy their company. The fact that they have a different *experience* may also introduce you to perspectives you had not encountered and challenge presumptions you never knew you possessed. There is darkness in *all* of us. What is your particular brand? I'm sure that would be very interesting indeed."

"What have you done with my son? Where is he?"

"Shut up! Listen. Don't talk."

Jack remained silent.

"Good," said Judith, easing herself into a battered seat opposite him. Her eyes were tunnelling right into Jack's as she spoke. "I'm going to tell you a story. A bedtime story to scare. Are you sitting comfortably, Mister Calvert?"

Chapter Thirty-Nine

"You may house their bodies, but not their souls . . ."
Kahlil Gibran, *The Prophet*

"ANY MORE ON those two bodies, Shaw?" asked Benson impatiently, sounding slightly irritated. Jack's remarks on the phone mystified him. He kept going over the short conversation, again and again, until he drew a blank. Perhaps all the strain of Adrian's disappearance was beginning to take its toll. It couldn't be easy, especially after Linda's death.

Guilt was gnawing at Benson. He should have called on Jack more often, gone fishing like they use to do. But instead he had deserted him—just like the rest of his so-called friends.

Shaw was leaning over a table, his eyes firmly embedded in a microscope. He appeared deaf to Benson's question.

Ignorant old bastard, thought Benson, standing at least six feet away from the cadavers stretched out on trolleys. To his nostrils, the distance felt like six inches. The stench was insufferable and the enclosed quarters only strengthened the smell. It was difficult to tell whether the bodies were adults or teenagers. The clothes were no help. They looked like painted-on tar, meshed with muck and rotted leaves.

Creatures had feasted joyously on the faces of the two bodies, the harsh winter granting the animals a wondrous appetite. Benson shuddered involuntarily, as if a million insects had just crawled over his body. The cadavers' horrendous condition reminded him of his own mortality. Despite all his macho bluster, Harry Benson dreaded death, the thought that one day that grumpy old bastard, Shaw, would be poking around his hairy hole, slicing and dicing like a chef preparing a banquet for Hell.

Boldly removing a cigarette from its packet, Benson placed it in his mouth. He fumbled in his pockets for his untrustworthy lighter. "How the hell can you stand the stench in here? Give me a good open-air killing any day." The unlit cigarette jerked in his mouth. He couldn't find the lighter, and was becoming more desperate in his searching.

If Shaw heard, he did not respond—not immediately. A few seconds later, he glanced up from the microscope and squinted his eyes, as if sunlight had touched them.

"Why are you always so hungry for conversation?" asked Shaw dismissively. "As soon as I find something relevant, you will be the first to know—oh, and don't even attempt to light that thing. This is a no-smoking area."

"Are you serious?" asked Benson, reluctantly returning the cigarette to its home. He knew he shouldn't have come down here, into Shaw's domain, to be spoken to like that, but something in Jack's voice had bothered him—the entire conversation had bothered him—and if it meant humbling himself in front of Shaw for a lead, then so be it.

Shaw's eyes returned to the microscope, much to Benson's annoyance.

"Can't you pull yourself away from that thing for one minute, you nasty old fuck?" said Benson. "I spoke to Jack on the phone, less than ten minutes ago. It just didn't sound right.

He didn't make sense. He was incoherent. Kept calling me John."

"That must have been nice for you," replied Shaw, finally easing away from the microscope, rubbing his tired eyes.

"Have you checked dental records?" Benson cleared his throat with a loud, deliberate cough. "Do . . . do you think one of the bodies . . . do you think one of them could be Adrian?"

When Shaw didn't answer, it put Benson on a war footing. "It's okay, you hiding away down here, not having to trek through all the shit out there, in the real world. The rest of us are doing our best to locate Jack's son. What the fuck are you doing, Shaw? Playing the mad scientist?"

Sighing, Shaw stood, and then walked a couple of feet to the trolleys. A few seconds later, he gently removed the covering sheets, exposing fully the bodies beneath. It was a tender, delicate movement and Benson understood immediately that no matter how much death or how many bodies this grumpy old bastard had witnessed, he still retained a modicum of respect for the dead.

"Come closer," said Shaw. "They won't bite. I promise."

"I'm fine, where I am," said Benson.

"You'll not be able to see anything from that distance. I want to show you something, up close and personal."

Reluctantly, Benson moved his feet in front of each other, until he stood perilously close to the two bodies. For one horrible, heart-stopping moment, he had a vision, a vision that the bodies were his and Jack's, sprawled out in some godforsaken landfill, a banquet for rats and insects. Finally, able to summon a few words, he asked, "Well? What is it?"

Shaw stared directly into Benson's eyes. "Post mortems are a slow process owing to the necessity for thoroughness. One mistake by me and the killer's mistake will never be discovered. Would you prefer the killer to escape justice because of your lack of patience? You think I don't care about Jack's son? Of course I damn well do. But unlike you, I can't afford the luxury of being so irritatingly transparent."

"I . . . well," mumbled Benson, caught off-guard by Shaw's outburst.

"For your information, both bodies were dumped, semi-buried within close proximity of each other—though at different times. The condition of this particular body"—Shaw pointed at the smaller of the two, with his index finger—"tells me that this was the first to be buried. Most of the skin is gone—caused by the elements and forest dwellers. Once the warmer weather arrived, the ice began to melt, pushing the bodies closer to the main stretch of water, allowing the fish to nibble and feast."

"Fish? The ones in Alexander Lake?"

"Where else?"

Benson felt his stomach heave. Just a few weeks ago, he had done some late-night ice fishing, catching at least ten well-fed fish. The subsequent days saw him devour all ten. It made him wonder if more than fish had entered his mouth.

"Fish can be quite carnivorous when the occasion arises," stated Shaw.

"Can we stop talking about fish?" asked Benson, believing he saw a ghost of a smile appear on Shaw's lips.

"Very well, but let me show you something before you throw up all over my floor."

Skilfully, Shaw dropped an object into a cleaning cloth. Little twists of his wrists and he appeared happy with the results, removing most of the darkened layer from the item.

"What is it?" asked Benson, slightly weary.

"Hold out your hand," commanded Shaw, a teacher about to administer the cane to a naughty pupil.

Obediently but reluctantly, Benson complied, stretching out his massive hand while Shaw deposited something in it. The item felt strangely cold, yet warm and bizarrely disconcerting.

"What the hell is—?" Before he could say the last word, Benson knew exactly what is was; believed beyond a doubt the identity of its owner stretched out before him. His stomach did a little flip-flap and suddenly all of Jack's words were coming back to him, clear as crystal, making him feel foolish and angry that he hadn't known their relevance until it was too late. Far too late, he feared.

I shouldn't be long, John . . . Long John . . .

Like a charging rhino, Benson ran through the doors, and up the first two flights of stairs, leaving a bewildered Shaw staring at the flapping doors.

Benson had never been fit, and over the last few years had piled on pounds of extra fat, lying to himself that, once retirement came, he would have plenty of time to get into shape.

He reached the third flight of stairs, out of breath, feeling dizzy, sweating like cheese. His heart was pounding mercilessly in his chest, sending tiny bolts of electricity up his left arm. He rested his back against a wall, desperately trying to obtain an intake of air, managing only to slither down the wall, unceremoniously, on to his large arse, as he felt his face redden and swell like a red balloon being given too much air.

Get up, you fat waste of space. Do something right for a change. Stop fucking moaning . . .

Sucking in beautiful air, Benson willed himself to stand and crash through the barrier of pain like a whale surfacing from the sea. Within seconds, he had slammed through the doors of Wilson's office, startling the superintendent.

"What the hell! What do you think you're doing, barging in like this, Benson?" asked Wilson, quickly regaining his composure, shuffling papers at the desk.

"It's Jack, Superintendent. He's in danger." Benson sucked in the stale, smoky air. "I believe he's gone to the Grazier place. He thinks . . . he thinks his son is there, held by Jeremiah Grazier and Joe Harris, our main suspects in the—"

"I warned Calvert to keep his nose out of police work. I also warned *you* about getting involved with him."

"Yes, yes, I know, you do a lot of warning. Right now, Superintendent, I couldn't give a monkey's tit about your warnings. I need permission to get a chopper into the air immediately."

Momentarily taken aback, Wilson simply stared at Benson.

"I would be very careful of how you speak to me, Detective Benson. Your retirement is coming very—"

"The chopper. *Now.*"

Wilson fluffed himself up like a peacock.

"There will be no chopper. Not now; not *ever.* Calvert can stew in his own mess. Now, I advise you to turn—"

Leaning over the desk, Benson forced his face in towards Wilson's. "If anything should happen to Jack Calvert, I will hold you personally responsible, you desk-eating piece of cowardly shit. I'm going to make sure every newspaper in the country knows that you had a vendetta against him because you were envious of his courage, while you for the last twenty years hid behind a desk, brown-nosing your way up the fucking ladder. Now, do I get that chopper or not?"

"Get out! You're finished here, just like your friend! I'll make sure that both you and—"

Benson slammed the door, shaking wood and glass, before making his way towards the front exit.

"Sir?" a young voice called after Benson, trailing behind him.

Benson ignored it until its owner caught up with him, tapping his back.

"*What?*" snarled Benson.

"I'm . . . I'm Johnson, sir. You saved me from being dismissed from the force, last week."

"Johnson? Oh, Starsky. Where's your shadow, Hutch?"

"Taylor, sir. He's been given traffic duty for two months."

"Rightly so. Next time, neither of you will be so fucking lucky. Anyway, nice chatting. Now, if you don't fucking mind, I'm in a hurry."

"I couldn't help overhearing the . . . conversation you had with Superintendent Wilson, sir."

"Couldn't you? Worth the watching, aren't you? Well?"

"I think . . . I think I can be of assistance to you, sir."

"What? You be of assistance to me? What are you mumbling about? Spit it out, lad."

"Fly, sir. I know how to fly."

For the first time in days—weeks, possibly—Harry Benson smiled. It was a fatherly smile.

"I always said you young cops could teach us old dogs a few tricks. Let's go, lad."

Less than ten minutes later, Benson and Johnson were airborne, though the older cop was wondering what he had walked into, feeling the chopper jerk a few times in midair.

"Are you sure you know how to fly this thing, Johnson?"

"Yes, sir. I've been taking flying lessons, in a light aircraft."

"A light . . . for fuck's sake . . . just keep your eyes on the road—or whatever it is you're supposed to keep them on up here."

The chopper narrowly avoided hitting the roof of a nearby factory, before panning away from the city entirely. A few minutes later, it eventually steadied—as did Benson.

"You know, you're going to be in the shit with Superintendent Wilson, taking me to the air, lad, going against his orders?"

"No, sir. I didn't hear Superintendent Wilson's orders. I was just obeying *yours.*"

Benson smiled. "Crafty sort of bastard, aren't you?"

"Yes, sir."

Chapter Forty

"Ultimate horror often paralyses memory in a merciful way."
H.P. Lovecraft, *The Rats in the Walls*

"I NEVER KNEW my parents, having spent most of my life in an *orphanage*. Orphanage? Another euphemism. Prison, a more truthful word," said Judith, so softly that Jack could barely make out the words. "The man in charge of that particular hellhole was called Albert Miles. Or, as the children in his custody called him, Mister Spittle." Judith's lip curled slightly, as if she were smelling sour milk. "Not a day passed that we didn't endure some sort of abuse—mainly sexual, from the *respected* Mister Spittle." She reached her hand into the cage and, like a magician, produced another rabbit. "Mister Spittle was just beautifully handsome in an almost delicate way, the kind of man you could almost call pretty, a gentleman to his friends and loving family. Oh, how he loved that family." A muscle in her pale face flitted for a moment. Her eyelids drooped half shut while her eyes went flat. She gripped the rabbit, tighter. "I can still see him, every night, undoing his belt buckle, allowing his greasy trousers to slide down his bony legs." The rabbit dangled, twitching violently on invisible strings. She opened its stomach, making it suffer horribly while it squirmed in her hand. It stopped once she slit its throat.

Judith stared at Jack, challengingly, almost daring him to say a word. Something was happening to her eyes. They were becoming clearer, as if a curtain had been removed. They were morphing into someone else's.

The eyes. Where have I seen them? In the wedding photos in Harris's cottage, yes; but some place else. Think . . .

"Do you know why we called him Mister Spittle? He had to spit on his hand to smooth his entry into our arses, did Mister Spittle. Sometimes, when he was drunk, he didn't even bother to try and wet our arses, always taking us from behind, like a purse-snatcher."

The eyes. Think, you stupid bastard. Think . . .

"Mister Spittle bred rabbits as a hobby, donating them to the 'Save the Orphans Organisation'." An eerie-sounding laugh jumped from Judith's throat. "Every Saturday night, he put on a show for some of the *selected* children in the orphanage, forcing them to watch rabbits fuck one another. He called me his little rabbit, did Mister Spittle—his sweet little rabbit whose sweating skin resembled stardust. Said he would teach me how to fuck like one." Dropping the dead rabbit at her feet, Judith reached for another. "'There is nothing so sweet as a child of pliant age,' he would whisper into my ear, as he forced his cock into me, from behind, pulling on my ears like a bunny rabbit."

The eyes. Oh, dear lord . . .

Now he remembered. Jack tried desperately to stop the blood rising in his head. It was throbbing, uncontrollably, like the warning of a volcano about to erupt. "You . . . you're the little boy, in the photographs . . . the little boy with the tortured eyes."

Chapter Forty-One

"... one must have the courage to dare."
Fyodor Dostoevsky, *Crime and Punishment*

JOHNSON HOVERED THE chopper near the edge of the Graziers'
land, instructed by Benson to do so.

"Little point in reducing the element of surprise, Johnson.
I'm sure the Graziers have heard us, anyway," said Benson, scanning the vastness of the land with his binoculars. *But what if
there is no surprise? What if I'm wrong? What if Jack isn't here—
never was?*

The chopper slumped suddenly like a slate falling from a
roof.

"Easy, lad," growled Benson, grabbing the passenger seat
tightly while his stomach parked somewhere in his throat. "This
isn't a bloody video game."

"Sorry, sir. I was only trying to get the chopper to—"

"There!" yelled Benson, relief pouring through. "Down
there, to the left. That's Jack's car. I'd know that piece of junk
anywhere. Even from up here, it's a bloody eyesore."

The car had been left stranded, beside a hill, hiding itself
close to the battered pathway leading directly on to the Graziers'
land.

"Oh yes." Benson smiled, picturing Jack, binoculars in hand, taking the advantage afforded him by the hill's height. "You sneaky old bastard, Jack."

"Should I go in first, sir, once we land? I topped the performance league at the Academy's shooting competition."

"Did you indeed? Well, these aren't cardboard cut-outs that we're after, lad. These bastards can shoot back. No, you just follow my instructions. No heroics. Play this right, and we'll both be tucked in our beds, tonight, safe and sound. Everything by the book. Understand?"

"Anything you say, sir," said Johnson.

"By the bloody book," reiterated Benson.

Chapter Forty-Two

"We come out of the dark and go into the dark again . . ."
Thomas Mann, *The Magic Mountain*

JUDITH DID NOT acknowledge Jack's statement about the photos, simply continued talking. "Night after night, Mister Spittle would force himself on the little rabbit. The little rabbit couldn't breathe. Would no one help? Do they hate the little rabbit that much? Please. Someone, somewhere, help. But no one ever listened—especially Mister Spittle's loving wife and children. Even God shut his eyes when it suited. Oh, the little rabbit learned a lot in that fucking hellhole."

"I can't even begin to imagine the horror of what you and the rest of the children must have gone—"

"Talking. Talking fucking talking! You *are* correct: you could *never* imagine the horror, Mister Talking Policeman. How can you imagine having your cock and balls pulled so hard, that they are damaged beyond repair, useless, like a eunuch's and that only a sex change can save you? Perhaps if I cut off *your* cock and balls, then you could begin to *imagine?*"

Jack grimaced.

Shaking her head, Judith continued. "How can you begin to *imagine* what it's like to be raped at will by an upstanding and respected member of the community, day in and day out, thinking it's all your fault, that you must have done some terrible thing in the life before and that this is God's punishment for it? No, you can *never* imagine."

A couple of rabbits whispered in the darkness. The old freezer hummed. It sounded like it was ready to give up the ghost. It sounded like it was whispering, also.

"You are right. One hundred per cent," said Jack. "I only hope that the perpetrator was arrested, and finally brought to justice. I believe people like that need to be put away for a very long time, never to be allowed to commit their evil acts again. I truly do."

Judith looked beyond Jack when she spoke, her eyes glazed, as if looking at a film being shown on the opposite wall.

"Justice? There is no such animal, Mister Truly Do."

"There are other conduits, Judith. The proper authorities—"

"So, it's Judith, now, Mister Calvert?" Judith smirked. "Trying the Stockholm syndrome? Don't waste your time. Are you familiar with the work of Artemisia Gentileschi, her rape?"

Jack nodded, slightly. "Yes."

"Then you know what happened to Artemisia when she brought the charge to the *proper authorities?*" hissed Judith, disdainfully. "The so-called trial was a painful public humiliation for Artemisia. During the proceedings, she underwent vaginal examination and torture with thumbscrews, to establish the veracity of her evidence. She was accused of being unchaste when she met Tassi, and also of promiscuity. But even the male-dominated court had no other choice once the mountain of evidence was produced and came tumbling down on top of them. Tassi was found guilty. He was given the choice of five years' hard labour or exile from Rome. He opted for the latter, but was back in Rome within four months. Was that *justice?*"

"No, of course not."

"The heroines of Artemisia's art are powerful women exacting revenge on male evildoers. Do you recall what Judith did to the Assyrians' military general, Holofernes, once she had seduced him in the tent?"

A stone of fear moved in Jack's stomach, sliding downwards like acid. He could feel hot blotches blooming on his neck. He wanted badly to scratch the blotches, dig his nails deep into them.

"Yes, I know the story."

"When I met Mister Spittle, *deliberately,* years later, in a downtown bar, he didn't recognise me in my new body, even though he more than anyone had contributed to my sex change." Judith smiled bitterly. "His wife had left him—*belatedly*—and he was nothing more than a lonely old perv. Do you know, he still kept all the photos of me and the other unfortunates, wrapped in tiny shoe boxes, just like the prisoners we were, all those years ago?" Sweat and snot pooled over Judith's upper lip. She did not attempt to wipe it.

The noise in the shed, for Jack, was suddenly becoming unbearable. The rabbits were screaming louder, smelling the blood of their butchered comrades. They sounded like a million children in orphanages, screaming for help. Help that would never come. The freezer, seemingly not to be outdone, hummed even louder, like a dentist's drill in Jack's teeth.

"I took Mister Spittle back here, to my house, and made him strip, filling his head with all manner of sexual perversion. He confided in me that he couldn't have normal sex, but I reassured him that after that night, he would never have to worry about that again." Judith was breathing heavily, as if performing a seance, or a bizarre exorcism. "I bent him over the bed, fondling his cock, getting him as hard as the steel rod in my other hand. His arse resisted for a while and I had to use my finger, initially, just to start the wonderful journey. That did the trick. He loved that little part, I think, just between you and me, but little did he know that soon he would have more than a little finger poking in there. I was even generous in my use of spittle before I rammed the steel rod home, watching his spine straighten with the pain." She was breathing heavier now, her bare breasts swelling abnormally. "I should have had a camera, just for old times' sake, for posterity, when the coldness of the cut-throat touched his hot sac, startling him even further. Then I whispered in his ear how his skin glistened like stardust—I will never forget the look on his face at those words, or the sound he made staring at his balls on the floor, as he grasped, too late, that the coincidence of our meeting was not chance, but an inevitable consequence of a desire for revenge."

Jack's gun rested two feet away, almost invisible between the rabbits' bloody carcasses. Controlling his breathing, he now felt a calmness slowly oozing through his body.

Keep staring at her, but picture your gun; keep it firmly in your head. Shoot Jeremiah first—wound if possible. Take the chance with the razor, not the shotgun.

Judith rose, and then stretched leisurely, like a drugged cat. Weirdly, her naked body—now moist with blood—shimmered with the gentle texture of a soft, carved pebble.

Walking towards the humming freezer, she opened its lid, its pale, jaundiced light blinding her momentarily like a vampire at sunrise.

"I was surprised at how easily his cock and balls gave way to the blade—a bit disappointed, actually. I thought there would have been more resistance, even though the shop assistant had informed me that the razor had a near-surgical cutting blade." She shrugged her shoulders before dipping into the freezer, the tiny stepping-stones of her spine arching a perfect "c". "Thankfully, this was more challenging . . ."

Jack was winded as it hit him smack up the balls. Only pride prevented him from buckling in pain.

Mister Spittle's head rested contently between Jack's legs, like an egg in a nest. Belatedly, Jack's body responded before his mind registered, shoving the ghastly item away, kicking at it, wildly.

"Filthy bastard!" he shouted, hating himself for allowing her to shock him. Rage was simmering under his powerlessness.

"Filthy bastard, indeed," Judith grinned. "See how old Spittle went for your cock, after all these years in the freezer? Told you he was a perv, didn't I?"

Jack was tiring, mentally and physically, draining of all emotion. Had he detected a softening in Judith's voice, an understanding that he had full sympathy with her, that all he wanted to know was that his son was safe and well? But the ugly, honest, rational part of his brain, the part that gives open appraisals and realistic predictions, the part that no one likes to acknowledge—that little voice was now laughing at him, telling him that he would have to make his move soon if he wanted to live. Better to die trying than to be slaughtered like one of the hapless rabbits. He hadn't come this far simply to have his head removed, to see the inside of a freezer.

"Albert Miles may have deserved his fate, but the little McTier girl, Nancy—what harm had she done? Why was she killed?" asked Jack, control slowly coming to his voice.

"Nancy was a beautiful, pigeon-plump, utterly delicious little lady, but bloodthirsty in the way that all little girls are. She loved to watch as I cut the rabbits," said Judith. "To my surprise, I did have feelings for her but I had to remain focused, knowing that the sins will be visited upon the sons and daughters."

"But . . . why? What did she do to deserve such a terrible death?"

"She did nothing. It was her grandfather, the *good* Doctor John McTier. But he wouldn't have cared less about me killing him. I needed to hurt him in a very bad way." Judith seemed in a trance before she spoke, again. "McTier was the doctor at the orphanage. He saw what went on, all the rapes and beatings, but did nothing. He also enjoyed his private viewing every Saturday night at the orphanage, along with the other good citizens of the town."

"Viewing?" asked Jack, the question long ago answered by his own speculation.

Judith smirked. "I have a sneaking suspicion you already know, Mister Calvert, but I'll humour you, anyway. Spittle made a small fortune with his nightly showings of children being raped. They were all there, the pillars of the community, the ghouls, the bad, and the ugly: Dickey Toner, John McTier, and quite a few others. There was a cop, also—though he may not have participated, as such. He had more interest in backhanders."

"A cop?" Jack's adrenalin flowed a notch quicker. "Who . . . what was the cop's name?"

Judith shrugged. "He remained faceless, collecting his payments away from prying eyes, only the stench of his cigars leaving fingerprints floating in the air."

"Are you sure he was a cop? Did you hear his voice, anything to recognise him by?"

"Just his stench and fat silhouette, but I have a feeling in my bones that I will meet him one day, soon. He was shrewd enough, doing most of his dealings with the owner of the Graham building, Peter Bryant."

"Bryant . . .?"

"I thought that would get your attention." Judith smiled. "Your whore friend's father owned the Graham building and surrounding area. The bastard died of cancer, a few years ago, making it impossible for me to have my pound of flesh, or to extract any relevant information about his cop friend. Fortunately, his daughter was able to pay."

"It was you on the phone, wasn't it?"

Judith ignored his question.

Jack licked his dry lips. "All . . . all I ask, Judith, is that you tell me what happened to my son. You of all people should have an understanding of what I'm going through. I'm a proud man, but I'm begging you, tell me something, anything. Please. I can help you."

"Help *me*? Where was all the help when I—*we*—needed it? The only one who ever tried to help me was a boy called Michael Wainwright, imprisoned in the same hellhole as me. Michael vowed always to protect me, no matter what. He attacked Mister Spittle, one night, after I had been raped . . ." Judith's voice trailed. "Spittle murdered him, buried him in the grounds of the orphanage. Spittle wasted no time informing me that I would join Michael in that cold hole in the ground if I resisted any further."

Jack's heart gave a little lurch. He wondered if Judith had heard the sound. There was little doubt in his head that it was a chopper, coming in to land.

"But Spittle was wrong," continued Judith. "He hadn't killed

Michael. Michael was too strong for him, and escaped after feigning his death. I knew that in my heart, and knew that one day he would come back to me, love me forever, protect me always."

The light was closing in behind Judith, and her shadow fell on Jack, but even in the dullness, he could see that she was considering him, washing her ink-blue eyes across his face. Deciding.

No longer hearing the chopper's sound, Jack wondered if he had imagined it; if it had ever really been there.

Standing slowly, Judith secured Jack's gun as she did so. "Personally, I have nothing against you . . . Jack. But you must understand that I cannot allow you to interfere with justice. I can't allow you to harm those whom I love. Please allow me to introduce you to Michael, my hero . . ."

Jack craned his head slowly, as directed, and tried to speak. No words came.

Adrian's eyes were huge in the frame of his sunken face, wide and vacant, like a window forced open. He was barely recognisable as the young boy who had fled into the storm. He held the shotgun inches from Jack's face.

It shocked Jack, Adrian's state, and he gasped inwardly as he felt the muzzle of his own gun being placed against the back of his head, the heaviness of the trigger hitting home as Judith pulled the trigger.

At that exact moment, everything around him seemed removed, hardly real. There were words in his head. There was a gap, a delay between the moment he heard the words and when he finally understood them.

Then the explosion came.

Chapter Forty-Three

*"Death never takes the wise man by surprise; he is always
ready to go there."*
Jean de la Fontaine, *Fables*, Book 8

IN A SPLIT-SECOND judgment, Benson had fired, just as Judith
fired the first chamber in Jack's gun. Benson did not ask
Judith to drop the gun. He did not ask her to surrender. He did
not give her a second chance to pull the trigger.

The shotgun blast hit Benson, slamming him violently
against the door of the shed, filling him with disbelief that his
godson could have done such a thing.

"Drop it!" shouted Johnson, tumbling to the ground, his
finger already squeezing the trigger, the gun aimed directly at
Adrian's head.

Jack leapt, adrenalin and instinct guiding him, pushing
Adrian to the floor, knocking the shotgun from his hands.

"You murdered her!" screamed Adrian, over and over again,
punching and kicking Jack.

Seconds later, Johnson stood over Adrian, gun primed.

"Don't!" shouted Jack. "He's . . . he's my son . . . don't shoot
. . . please don't shoot."

"Johnson . . . do . . . do as Jack says . . . lad. It's . . . it's over
. . ." groaned Benson.

While Johnson cuffed Adrian, Jack hastily knelt beside Benson, ripping his own shirt, hoping to stop the frightening flow
of blood. The burly cop's enormous chest had taken most of the
blast. A large napkin of blood stained the top half of it.

"Easy, Harry," whispered Jack, desperately trying to staunch
the flow.

Benson's tongue darted in and out, trying to capture air.

"It . . . it wasn't his fault . . . Jack . . . Adrian . . ." Pink blood
bubbled at the side of Benson's mouth. "Should . . . I should
have known better . . . fucking cavalry charges, at my age. You
. . . should always go by . . . the fucking book."

"Easy . . . easy, Harry. Don't talk. Help is on its way . . . we'll
use the chopper. You'll be in hospital in no time."

Benson forced a smile. Another pink bubble appeared at the
side of his mouth, followed by a spurt of blood. "If . . . you're
daft enough . . . to take that chopper, trust me, you . . . you *will*
end up in hospital."

Benson's fingers worked their way into his coat pocket,
returning a few seconds later.

"Here . . . take this." Benson squeezed Grazier's glass eye into
Jack's hand. "That fucker Grazier . . . saved . . . your life . . .
Shaw . . . Shaw found it on Grazier's body . . . I . . . didn't catch
on to that . . . Long John shit . . . on the phone . . . till Shaw
handed me that . . . glass fucking eye . . ." Blood was flowing
more fluently now. "The bodies . . . in Barton's Forest . . . Grazier and Harris . . . throats cut . . ."

"Don't talk, Harry. Save your strength. You'll need it for all
that fishing we're going to do."

"Stop making me . . . laugh . . . it hurts my ribs." Benson

attempted a smile. "Promise . . . promise you'll . . . say nothing about . . . the car crash . . . if you don't promise . . . I'll come back . . . and fucking haunt you . . ."

"Stop talking like that, you old bastard. You are *not* going to die on me. Do you hear me? I will not allow you to—"

"*Promise!*" hissed Benson, through clenched teeth. "That bastard Wilson . . . would take Anne's . . . police pension . . . promise me . . ."

"I . . . I promise, Harry, I promise . . ." Jack allowed the blood to flow freely now. There was little point in trying to halt it. "Adrian didn't mean to shoot you, Harry. You know that, don't you? His head is all fucked up. Harry? Can you hear me, Harry . . .?"

Benson's eyes stared up at his ex-partner, his best friend. He didn't answer.

Chapter Forty-Four

*"Personally, I have no bone to pick with graveyards, I take the air
there willingly, perhaps more willingly than elsewhere,
when take the air I must."*
Samuel Beckett, *First Love*

THE RAIN SOFTENED the soil along the graveyard, adjacent to the Graham building, making the task of the mechanical digger a lot easier. For such a metal monstrosity, the digger moved delicately, almost pawing the soil before interrupting it.

Watching the digger, Jack became almost hypnotised by its movement mingling with the sound of falling rain on his umbrella.

"Are you listening to me?" asked Shaw.

"What? Sorry . . . my mind was elsewhere."

"I said Wilson would never have authorised this exhumation. Too much manpower and overtime money wasted, for his mentality. It was a godsend, his unexpected resignation. Don't you think?"

Jack detected just a hint of curiosity in Shaw's voice. Everyone was speculating on Wilson's sudden vocation for civilian life. Rumour was rife—something to do with the Graham building and protection money, and a can of worms spilling on to the streets, crawling all over town. Local politicians' names were being whispered. A judge and a member of the clergy had already been taken in for questioning by the police. Only Jack Calvert held the secret, for now. But soon the worms would find their way into the homes of so-called respected citizens, and into the mouth of William Wilson and his cronies.

The digger stopped abruptly, indicated to do so by one of Shaw's assistants. Less than a minute later, a small, badly dilapidated box was removed.

"They couldn't even grant the children a respectable burial," whispered Shaw, surprising Jack with the emotion in his voice. "Too many bodies, Calvert. I'm afraid we've unearthed more than death in this wretched patch of earth."

"When you live in a place, it becomes you whether you want it to or not, Shaw. We are all guilty of whatever this burial ground accuses us of. Each and every one of us."

Shaw looked away from the digger. "When you didn't show up for Benson's funeral, it caused a bit of a stir. But as I listened to Wilson's last official speech about Benson's bravery, I realised you wouldn't have been able to control yourself. You did the right thing."

Jack laughed bitterly. "The right thing? I wouldn't know the right thing if it slapped me about the face. I'm no better than Wilson, Shaw. Make no mistake about that."

The rain was falling in brown streaks, as if washing all the filth from the sky's crust. Jack felt despondency seep in as the rain soaked through his clothes, chilling his bones.

"How is your son? You understand that it will take time and patience? Fortunately, there is a lot of help nowadays."

Jack shuddered involuntary. He wanted to go home, but needed to talk to someone, someone with answers and explanations.

Walls were never good listeners, despite what the old war posters proclaimed.

"Murder charges have been reduced to involuntary manslaughter. I'm waiting to hear if he will be released on bail until the trial. All I can do is hope that eventually all charges will be dropped. It wasn't Adrian who fired those shots. It was drugs and the brainwashing." Jack looked away from Shaw. "I don't know . . . I don't know if he will ever be the same, sullied by such an experience and knowledge of evil . . . what he saw, what he went through. In times like this, I would have whispered a tiny prayer to God, but if this case has taught me one thing, it's that God never did exist."

The agnostic Shaw said nothing for a while. He appeared transfixed in his own world of the dead, as he watched the digger vomit up more soil and potential revelations.

"How is Miss Bryant? Thank goodness the newspapers were willing to print the red herring that she was fatally wounded."

"I never thought I'd be grateful to any newspaper," acknowledged Jack. "Sarah will need major surgery on her face. They still can't tell me if she will ever regain the full use of her legs. The doctor said she was *lucky*. Time will tell what his definition of being lucky is."

"I completed a toxicology test on the remains of both Jeremiah Grazier and Joseph Harris, yesterday. They had both been poisoned—though in different ways. Harris's stomach revealed vitamin tablets laced with cyanide. He consumed a large quantity of alcohol—probably whiskey—preceding administration of the cyanide. Both men had their throats cut, also, prior to death. Not a very gentle death at all," said Shaw.

Jack shuddered before sucking in a taste of dirty air. He dreaded asking Shaw the question, but had no other choice. "Do . . . do you think both murders were committed by one person? The same person? You don't think Adrian had anything to do with them?"

Almost tenderly, Shaw reached and touched Jack's shoulder. "It really doesn't matter what I think. My files on both deaths are now closed. Let us worry about the living, now. The dead can take care of themselves."

"Harris had nothing to do with any of this," said Jack. "We found the money he withdrew, along with his passport, in Grazier's cupboard. It looks as if they set him up, using him to take us off their trail. Poor bastard. Even the child porn magazines, conveniently found in Harris's cottage, were purchased by Jeremiah using his own credit card."

An assistant was waving, indicating that Shaw was needed over at the tent that constituted a makeshift headquarters.

"I'll call you if there are any further developments, Calvert," said Shaw, turning to go. "By the looks of things here, it's going to be a very long time before we get any answers. In the meantime, if you need anything, just give me a call."

Removing a photo from his pocket, Jack said, "There *is* one thing I would appreciate you doing for me. This belonged to Judith Grazier. It's a picture of a young boy called Michael Wainwright. He's in there, somewhere among the dead. I want you to find him. I want you to do this. Understand? It would mean a lot to me. I need to give him a decent burial."

Hesitantly, Shaw took the photo. "I'm not supposed to . . ." He sighed, looking from the photo to Jack. "I'll do my best to locate the subject . . . the boy's body."

"Despite all that she did, I can't help feeling sorry for her—for all those kids. The system failed, not only Judith, but literally hundreds of others, and I don't suppose we will ever know the exact number."

Shaw left, stumbling over the tiny hills of muck, cursing as he did so.

Fatigued, Jack turned and made his way across the sodden ground. Directly above, he could hear the sound of birds, crows, caw-caw cawing. Their sound was everywhere.

SOME OTHER READING
from

BRANDON

JACK BARRY
Miss Katie Regrets

From the Dublin's criminal underbelly comes a gripping story of guns, drugs, prostitution and corruption. At the centre of a spider's web of intrigue sits the enigmatic figure of Miss Katie, a crabby transvestite who will, under pressure, kiss and tell. And, perhaps, kill.

ISBN 0 86322 354 0; paperback original

KEN BRUEN (ED)
Dublin Noir

Nineteen previously unpublished stories by acclaimed crime writers, each one set in Dublin
Brand new stories by Ray Banks, James O. Born, Ken Bruen, Reed Farrell Coleman, Eoin Colfer, Jim Fusilli, Patrick J. Lambe, Laura Lippman, Craig McDonald, Pat Mullan, Gary Phillips, John Rickards, Peter Spiegelman, Jason Starr, Olen Steinhauer, Charlie Stella, Duane Swier-czynski, Sarah Weinman and Kevin Wignall.

ISBN 0 86322 353 2; paperback original

SAM MILLAR
The Redemption Factory

"While most writers sit in their study and make it up, Sam Millar has lived it and every sentence... evokes a searing truth about men, their dark past, and the code by which they live. Great title, great read. Disturbingly brutal. I enjoyed it immensely." Cyrus Nowrasteh

ISBN 0 86322 339 7; paperback original

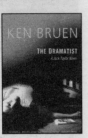

KITTY FITZGERALD
Small Acts of Treachery

"Mystery and politics, a forbidden sexual attraction that turns into romance; Kitty Fitzgerald takes the reader on a gripping roller coaster through the recent past. This is a story you can't stop reading, with an undertow which will give you cause to reflect." Sheila Rowbotham

ISBN 086322 297 8; paperback

J.S. COOK
A Cold-Blooded Scoundrel

An Inspector Devlin Mystery
In London, at a time when Jack the Ripper is still fresh in the memory, a well-known male prostitute is brutally murdered, the head neatly severed, and the body set on fire.

ISBN 0 86322 336 2; paperback original

EVELYN CONLON
Skin of Dreams

"A courageous, intensely imagined and tightly focused book that asks powerful questions of authority... this is the kind of Irish novel that is all too rare." Joseph O'Connor

ISBN 0 86322 306 0; paperback original

LARRY KIRWAN
Green Suede Shoes

"Lively and always readable. He has wrought a refined tale of a raw existence, filled with colorful characters and vivid accounts." *Publishers Weekly*

ISBN 086322 343 5; paperback original

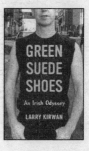